SONG

OF THE

BUFFALO

BOY

SONG

OF THE

BUFFALO

BOY

SHERRY GARLAND

Harcourt Brace Jovanovich, Publishers

San Diego   New York   London

FRANKLIN PIERCE
COLLEGE LIBRARY
RINDGE, N.H. 03461

HBJ

Copyright © 1992 by Sherry Garland

All rights reserved.
No part of this publication may be
reproduced or transmitted in any form or by any means,
electronic or mechanical, including photocopy, recording,
or any information storage and retrieval system,
without permission in writing from the publisher.

Requests for permission to make
copies of any part of the work should be mailed to:
Permissions Department,
Harcourt Brace Jovanovich, Publishers, 8th Floor,
Orlando, Florida 32887.

Library of Congress Cataloging-in-Publication Data
Garland, Sherry.
Song of the buffalo boy/by Sherry Garland — 1st ed.
p.   cm.
Summary: Shunned and mistreated because of her mixed heritage and
determined to avoid an arranged marriage, seventeen-year-old Loi
runs away to Ho Chi Minh City with the hope that she and the boy she
loves will be able to go to the United States to find her American
father.
ISBN 0-15-277107-7
[1. Amerasians — Fiction. 2. Vietnam — Fiction.] I. Title.
PZ7.G18415So   1992
[Fic] — dc20   91-31872

Designed by Trina Stahl

Printed in the United States of America

First edition
A B C D E

CURR
P2
7
.G18415
So
1992

To the
Children of All Wars

ACKNOWLEDGMENTS

This book would not have come to pass without the help of many people, and I would like to especially thank the following: the Society of Children's Book Writers and Judy Blume for awarding me a Works-in-Progress grant; my editor, Karen Grove, for her never-ending encouragement and guidance; all my Vietnamese friends who told me about the mother-land they love so dearly; and my husband, Clyde, who still believes there will come a day . . .

In addition, I found the following resources greatly valuable and inspiring: *Vietnam: My Country Forever* by Tran Cao Linh; *The Land I Lost: Adventures of a Boy in Vietnam* by Huynh Quang Nhuong; *When Heaven and Earth Changed Places* by Le Ly Hayslip; *Vietnam: Opening Doors to the World* by Rick Graetz; *Vietnam: The Land We Never Knew* by Geoffrey Clifford; *The Vietnam Guidebook* by Barbara Cohen; and *Flashbacks: On Returning to Vietnam* by Morley Safer.

SONG

OF THE

BUFFALO
BOY

PROLOGUE

THE LITTLE girl is sitting in the middle of a room on a hard, sticky floor, watching the American soldier. His blue eyes twinkle and his white teeth gleam as he picks her up. She feels herself going high, higher than his smiling face, higher than his curly hair, so high that she must catch her breath. She feels lighthearted, like a singing bird in the top of a tamarind tree rocking with the wind. Above her head a dusty, squeaky ceiling fan slowly whirls, stirring her brown hair, but she isn't afraid. The American soldier's big, strong hands have never dropped her before.

The child slips her fingers into his shirt pocket. There is always something good there. This time it is a red-and-white candy stick. But it isn't sweet like sugarcane. Its unfamiliar odor tickles her nose, and the strange taste tingles her mouth. The girl spits it out onto the front of her crisp red linen dress.

The child's mother crosses the room, wearing a blue *ao dai* with a golden phoenix embroidered on the front panel. She smells fresh and tangy, like ginger-blossom soap.

"Don't be such a rude little girl, Loi," Má says as she puts the candy back into her daughter's mouth. But Loi spits it out again. The soldier tilts his head back and laughs out loud before throwing the candy out the open window. Then he hugs Loi tightly and puts his lips on her cheek. Loi hates the wetness and rubs it off with her fist.

The soldier gently puts Loi down and speaks to her mother in a soft voice. He has to stoop very low to place his lips on her cheek. But Má doesn't wipe off the wetness. She bows a little, and her face looks pale.

A big frown wrinkles Loi's brow as she waits for the soldier to give her another treat. But he must have forgotten. He kneels in front of her and speaks in his strange language. The only words Loi understands are her name and "Má" and "good-bye." The man's voice is heavy and water fills his eyes. Then he reaches into his pocket, takes something out, and presses it into Loi's hands. She stares at a piece of thick, glossy paper with the image of the soldier, her mother, and a baby.

Loi is sitting on the dirty floor, studying this

strange piece of paper, which is not good for eating, when she hears the door close. When she turns around, the soldier is gone and her mother is crying. Loi decides to cry, too.

It is later now, at least two or three years. Loi knows this because Má's blue *ao dai* is faded and patched. And Loi is now tall enough to stand at the window and look down into the small garden behind the stained stucco building. The iron gate with a dragon's head on it is wide open, and strangers are digging up the vegetables like hungry rabbits.

Má doesn't seem to notice the strangers. She scurries about the room collecting their belongings. It only takes her a few minutes to stuff everything into an old pair of torn, baggy black pants and tie the legs into knots.

Má leads Loi by the hand down a long flight of stairs and into a narrow, dark alley. Out on the street people are running wildly; women and babies are screaming and crying. Loi squeezes her mother's fingers tighter and presses against her legs, trying to hide beneath the flaps of the faded *ao dai*.

When her mother tries to step out into the crowded street, a three-wheeled *cyclo* loaded with bundles rushes in front of them. Má cries out as one of the boxes bumps against her side and knocks her to the ground. Loi cries and tugs at Má's arm. A man in a white shirt and black slacks leans over and helps her mother up. The two adults speak too rapidly for Loi to understand. Then he swings Loi up to his shoulders.

She has seen this man before. He lives in the building next door and always wears the same white shirt and black slacks. But he never laughs like the tall American soldier did. Loi calls him Uncle, even though he is not really kin to her. It is what she calls all the grown-up men she knows.

People are running everywhere. Some carry big bundles on their backs or in baskets or hanging from *don ganh*s. Bicycles beep and *cyclo* drivers shout and curse as their pedals and wheels jam and lock against each other.

Loi begins to cry again, everything is in such confusion, but her mother tells her to hush. She says that Uncle is taking them to a safe place outside the city, so Loi doesn't cry anymore. She holds on to Uncle's neck. His hands aren't big like the blue-eyed soldier's hands were, but he is strong. He smells like rice and fish sauce, and it makes Loi remember that she only had one small bowl of *pho*, noodle soup, for breakfast early that morning. Her stomach is rumbling.

They push through the crowd. Trucks try to pass, loaded to the top with packages and furniture and people, but they can't move. As far as she can see, the road leading to the sea is jammed with bikes and trucks and people on foot.

Suddenly a loud boom like thunder cracks the air. The windows nearby shatter, and glass rains onto the street. A small boy screams and sits with his hands over his face while his mother lies beside him all quiet. The wind blows the flaps of her brown dress up over her face, but she doesn't move.

Another boom rapidly follows the first, and more glass crashes onto the avenue near them. Loi is trying very hard not to cry; she doesn't want to shame her mother. She bites her lip and tries to think of something else. But all that comes to her mind is the photo of the American soldier, which is safely hidden in a secret pocket inside her blouse.

Uncle leads them down an alley just as another boom shakes the earth under their feet. They tumble to the ground. Loi's knees sting with pain where the skin has scraped off. She smells smoke and looks around her. A yellow flame licks at the stucco walls of an old French bank building. People are running from it like ants in the garden after she has stirred their hill with a stick.

Uncle picks Loi up again. He holds her mother's hand tightly. Loi bobs up and down on Uncle's shoulders, he is running so fast. The hot wind whips her hair back from her flushed cheeks. All around them, fires crackle in the buildings, and soon cinders and pieces of soot begin to lodge in Loi's hair. Broken glass, bricks, and lumber clutter the streets, making it difficult for bicyclists and *cyclo* drivers to pedal by.

Here and there, people lie still in the middle of the street and women are crying.

Up ahead, Loi sees some soldiers in green-spotted uniforms blocking the intersection. Heavy guns are slung over their shoulders. No one can pass by without first speaking to them.

Uncle stops running and whispers to Má. Má's eyes grow wide and Loi can see her mother trembling. When they start to turn back, a soldier spies them and shouts. His sagging ammunition belt jingles as he walks toward them.

"Pay me money to get down the street," he says to Loi's mother. "If the Viet Cong find you and that half-breed *con-lai* baby, you'll be killed. Give me all your money."

"She doesn't have any money," Uncle says, but the soldier points the gun at Uncle and holds him back.

"Of course she does. All women who slept with American soldiers have money. Lots of money. Maybe he gave you gold and jade, too. Let me see."

The soldier grabs Má and rips the bodice of her blue *ao dai*. She screams, and Loi begins to cry. The soldier jerks a gold chain from Má's neck and pulls a ring from her finger. Another soldier cuts open the cloth bag and flings its contents into the street. He makes a pile of the things he wants.

Loi's mother tries to cover her naked chest with

her long hair so the other soldiers won't stare and laugh. Uncle curses. He puts Loi down and tries to kick the soldier. But the soldier hits him hard in the face with the rifle butt. Blood spills from Uncle's mouth and trickles down his chin and all over the front of his white shirt as he backs away.

"I have no money!" Má shouts. She falls to her knees. She bows low and rocks back and forth, crying. The soldier examines the gold necklace and then looks down at Loi.

"Fatherless *con-hoang!*" he snarls and spits into the street. "You'd better get out before the Viet Cong eat you for lunch." Then he laughs and pushes Má's face into a pile of wet garbage and walks away.

Loi runs to her mother and flings her arms around Má's neck. She can feel her mother's body shake with loud sobs.

"He took everything I owned," Má moans. "We have nothing now."

Loi looks at Má a long time, then remembers something. She reaches into her pocket and pulls out the photograph of the tall soldier with the blue eyes. It is bent and cracked now. She hands it to her mother.

Blinking her eyes, the woman stares at the picture, then she hugs Loi close. She squeezes so tightly that Loi can't breathe.

"Never show that picture to anyone! Never!" she

whispers in a hoarse voice. Then she throws the photo into the gutter at Loi's feet. But when she looks away, Loi picks it back up.

Uncle leaves and returns with a kitchen knife and a shirt for Loi's mother in his hand. He gives it to Má, and after putting the shirt on she quickly crops Loi's hair close to her head. Tears of shame sting Loi's eyes. Her mother always tells her that her hair is so pretty because it isn't as black or thick or straight as hers. It curls like tendrils on a pea vine and feels as soft as a kitten.

"Má, stop! Why are you cutting my hair?" Loi yells out, but her mother forces her to sit still until all the curls are lying on the street. Loi cannot stop the tears falling down her cheeks. How can she face the other children without hair? She must look so ugly now!

Then Uncle pushes a small *non-la* hat, the kind farmers wear, down over Loi's head. He ties the sash so tightly she can hardly swallow.

"If you want to stay alive, Loi, do not take this hat off, no matter what happens," Uncle warns her as he picks her up again. "You are a *con-lai*; you must never forget that."

I

THE SONG

LOI WAS dreaming about the American soldier again when she was awakened by the songs of the buffalo boys. She blinked a moment until the familiar sounds of morning chased the dream away.

Without even going to her window, Loi knew exactly what the boys looked like. Sitting atop their water buffaloes, bamboo switches in their hands, the boys were urging the slow-moving bovines down the path toward the grazing pastures.

And she knew each song as surely as she knew her own name. The brothers Thinh and Trung, who were very young, sang happy songs in small, shrill voices. Crazy Hai couldn't speak, but his bamboo flute trilled out a haunting melody that echoed across the misty fields. But the best song of all, the one that glowed as warm as the mid-autumn moon, belonged to Khai. Of all the songs, Khai's was the one that told a tale of true love; of all the songs, Khai's was meant for her.

Loi smiled to herself and curled her knees up closer to her chest. She knew it was time to get up. Soon the sun would stretch its rosy fingers over the jagged mountain peaks and spread its mellow light over the cluster of huts that seemed to float in a sea of golden rice.

But Loi wanted to stay curled up just a moment longer. Just until Khai's last sweet notes had echoed over the rice fields. Just until the dull clop-clop of cloven hooves on soft earth and the occasional bovine snort had faded away.

With a reluctant sigh, she sat up and stretched, brushing her fingertips against the hair of her youngest cousin, who lay asleep on the cot next to hers. How long had her arms been able to reach that far, she wondered. It seemed like only a year ago that her body fit neatly inside the confines of the thin straw mattress. Now her feet were hanging over the edge of her low cot.

Loi stared at her feet and ankles sticking out of the bottoms of the baggy black *quan* her mother had so carefully sewn for her over two years ago. It would be pointless to ask for another pair. Even after harvest, the family wouldn't have enough money for such luxuries as new cloth. And her mother would never dig into her cache buried in the yard except for an emergency. The best Loi could hope for would be an extra band added around the already-extended bottoms.

"Get up, idle girl!" Má's whisper broke into her thoughts. "Quickly, go fetch fresh water before Uncle Long wakes up."

Loi glanced across the hut at her uncle sleeping in the *nha tren*, the front of the house, near the family altar. She, along with her mother and three cousins, slept in the *nha duoi*, or back of the house, near the kitchen. Even her aunt, Uncle's wife, had slept there beside the children until she died.

Without speaking, Loi pushed the mosquito net away and took the *don ganh* pole down from the wall. She quietly lowered the notched palm-wood tree that served as a ladder. Every night she lifted it up into the hut so that wild animals would not get inside.

As she stepped down, something scampered across her feet. Probably rats. She didn't mind rats; she only wished she could see where they were. It was still dark, but already lanterns glowed softly inside a few huts. And in the distance, pink-gray light began to halo the jagged mountains.

Loi reached under the hut for two resin-lined water baskets, trying not to disturb the pigs sleeping there. She slipped an empty basket onto each end of the *giong*—strips hanging from the *don ganh*—and balanced the wooden pole across her shoulder. It felt as light as a feather as Loi trotted toward the community well.

Misty pockets of fog rose from the moist earth to cool her cheeks, and the dusty smell of ripened rice from the paddies blended with the tangy fragrance of citronella to tingle her nostrils. The peace and isolation made early morning Loi's favorite time of the day, and now that the nights were becoming a little cooler and the rainy season was nearing its end, she felt a great relief.

There was one bad thing about this time of the year. But then she had long ago noticed that nearly all good things have a bad side, like a rose has its thorns. She loved the autumn with its cooler nights and colorful festivals, but harvesting was backbreaking work. And worst of all, harvesttime meant the arrival of Officer Hiep. The very thought of him made Loi shiver, and she tried to force his image from her mind.

As she padded lightly down the worn path at a steady rhythmic gait, listening to frogs leaping out of her way into the irrigation ditches, she prayed for two things. She prayed that there would be no snakes in the path, and she prayed that there would be no people at the well. This morning she did not feel she could bear the usual prying stares and unkind remarks about her looks or her height. Today she just wanted to think about standing beside Khai, cutting row after row of dried rice stalks, exchanging secret smiles and glances. She began to softly sing Khai's sweet buffalo song.

When she reached the well, only one person was there, a boy of about eighteen. Although Loi was one year younger than the boy, she towered over him. She stood to one side looking at the ground, waiting for him to finish. When he was through, she stepped up. He didn't offer to help her with the awkward water baskets and walked away without speaking.

Loi didn't mind; silence was her old friend.

She lowered the baskets one at a time until she heard soft splashes and felt the heaviness of water inside them. They were cumbersome to hoist, but her arms were strong and hard from years of lifting water baskets and bags of rice and bundles of firewood.

She slipped the baskets into the cradles of the *don ganh* and adjusted the wooden pole over her shoulder. Pain pressed into her neck and shoulder until she had balanced the weight. As she looped her arm around the front of the pole, she thought she heard her name.

"Loi!" a voice whispered from a clump of tall elephant grass.

"Who's there? Khai? Is it you?" Her heart began to beat fast.

The grass quivered and Khai stepped into the clearing. Rosy light streaked over his smooth face and lean, straight body. The early-morning breeze ruffled the baggy black pants and tattered white shirt he always wore. His cone-shaped *non-la* hung loosely on his back. Loi glanced up and down the path to make sure no one saw them, for being alone with a young man was unacceptable. Then she deposited the baskets on the ground and stepped to his side.

"Khai, what are you doing here? You know your father would be angry if he saw you talking to me." She frowned and pretended to be angry herself but failed to convince him. His dark, sensitive eyes glistened in the pale light and his sweet smile warmed her heart.

"Yes, I know. But I had to give you this gift now, in case I don't get to speak to you again. We will be busy with the harvest for many days."

Khai removed a dark object from his pocket and pressed it into Loi's palm.

"It's beautiful," she whispered. Her dark liquid eyes grew larger and her heart puffed up with pride as she examined the piece of teakwood skillfully carved into the shape of a water buffalo. In the weak morning light, she couldn't see the finer details, but her fingers felt the smooth contours of the animal's broad shoulders, sharp backbone, and large horns swooping backward.

"I'm going to carve you a golden phoenix next," said Khai tenderly, "for good luck and happiness. I hope to go into the jungle for wood after harvest is over."

"The buffalo is perfect, Khai. I shall cherish it forever. But why haven't you put your initials on the bottom?"

Khai looked at the ground for a moment.

"I'm not good enough yet. Look at the horns—they're too small and the ridges are all wrong. And the poor animal's mouth is agape like a cave. I must practice many more years before I dare to put my name on any of my pieces."

Loi pointed a finger at his face.

"Vo Dinh Khai—why are you always putting yourself in such low esteem? No one else in the village carves as well as you do."

"Except for Great-grandfather Ngoc—he's the one who taught me."

"True. But his eyesight is gone now. You are his eyes and soul, he loves you so much, and you are the best carver. Why don't you try to sell your figurines at the market in Da Lat? I could take some with me when Má and I go to sell our vegetables. Your cousins are going to take baskets and Mrs. Tran is going to take her embroidery work to sell. I know you could make some money."

Khai shook his head slowly.

"My father thinks carving is a foolish waste of time. He thinks all things of beauty are useless and only mean trouble . . . Perhaps that is why he dislikes you so much, because of your beauty."

Loi turned away for a moment and felt heat flooding over her face. She bit her lip to keep from smiling, so he wouldn't think she was so vain as to care about compliments.

"Why do you call me beautiful, when all the other

15

villagers call me ugly and *con-hoang*—fatherless child? See, my hair is not as thick and straight and black as yours, and my eyes do not have the beautiful slant of yours. And my skin—how I detest these freckles on my nose! I want to look like you and your family. I hate being different." Loi plopped down on the edge of the well and stared at her hands in her lap. Even they were ugly—long and large, not tiny and delicately tapered like her mother's.

Khai frowned and crossed his arms as he sat beside her.

"Now who is the one putting herself in low esteem? How many times must I tell you that you are the most beautiful girl on earth to me—like a fairy from Mount Nam Nhuc."

A shy smile touched Loi's lips, and she could not resist poking Khai's folded arms. Though he was slender of build, his muscles were as hard as the piece of carved teak.

"And have you ever seen a fairy, Mr. Khai?"

"No, but neither have you. Perhaps all the fairies in the mountains have soft, curly brown hair. And freckles on their noses. How can we say for sure?"

Loi had to laugh out loud, but Khai's face remained so serious, she knew he really believed what he was saying.

"All right, Mr. Khai, if you persist in calling me beautiful, who am I to disagree? Is that correct?"

"Correct."

"Then, if I say that your carvings are excellent, who are you to disagree? Correct?" She wagged a finger before his face.

Khai grinned and shook his head. He tapped her on the nose.

"See, you *are* a fairy after all. You've tricked me already. But . . . shhh . . . I hear someone coming."

Loi stood and glanced down the trail. A young man was coming toward them carrying two water baskets.

"Oh no, it's your brother Quy!" Loi exclaimed. Quy was Khai's twenty-year-old brother, and he disliked Loi intensely. "Run, quickly. Perhaps I'll see you today in the fields. Try to walk near me if you can. I'll share my rice cakes at mealtime."

Khai touched her hand and disappeared back into the elephant grass. Loi adjusted the *don ganh* on her shoulder and started to trot for home. If she ran, perhaps Quy would say nothing. But luck was not with her, for as she stepped off the path to allow him to walk by, he called out.

"Who were you talking to just now, fatherless *con-lai?*"

How she hated that word, *con-lai!* As if she were some freakish half-breed offspring of a pig and a cow. And it reminded her too much of her dreams. She decided not to grace Quy with a reply and just stared at the ground.

"It better not have been my brother Khai," Quy

said in a voice loud enough to carry over to the quivering elephant grass. "He knows that Father forbids him to speak to you. Father and I have already chosen the perfect wife for Khai. A nice girl from a respectable family. My baby brother would have to be simpleminded to think we would allow him to ruin our honorable family name by marrying a *con-lai* whose mother slept with American soldiers for money."

Loi jerked her head up and felt the first beams of sunlight strike her moist eyes.

"Do not speak about my mother in such a tone. She did no such thing."

"Surely you don't expect anyone to believe that ill-conceived lie that your mother and your uncle insist on telling everyone."

"It is not a lie!"

"No? Now—how does the story go? Ah yes . . . your mother was supposedly molested by American soldiers while she was defending her country, and they forced themselves on her. We are expected to believe that?"

"If my mother says it is true, then it is."

"Ha! If the story were true, she would have tossed you into the river the moment you were born. Or better yet, she would have thrown herself into the river the moment the soldiers touched her, like any respectable woman would do."

A large, sharp lump rose to Loi's throat. When she tried to swallow it down and speak, a sob choked her words. All she could do was stare into his angry eyes. Then she heard footsteps behind her, and suddenly Khai was standing by her side.

"Please do not speak to Loi like that, older brother. She cannot help what her father is any more than you can help it that one of our cousins stole a water buffalo many years ago and was executed for theft."

"What a stupid comparison, little brother. That cousin was already dead before I was even born. What has it to do with me?"

"And, so, Loi's father returned to America before she could even speak. Why do you hate her so? What has she done to you?"

"Don't ask me such a foolish question. Ask our father who lost his crops and water buffaloes; ask your uncles who lost their eyes and limbs. Ask your aunt who weeps for six dead children. Ask all the heroes buried in graves with no names on them, far away from their ancestral villages. A man dares not go out at night for the dreadful moaning and wailing of their restless spirits."

Quy shoved a water basket into Khai's hands. He stared into his young brother's face for a long time, then sighed and shook his head. His eyes softened, and the anger slowly subsided.

"I guess you are too young and too simple to understand the answers they would give you anyway. Here, help me with the water before you go back to the buffaloes. And don't worry, your secret rendezvous here today is safe with me—for a while."

Then Quy turned to Loi, and his eyes grew hard again.

"If you want me to keep your secret, stay away from my brother. Look for a husband some other place. Perhaps a wild mountain *moi* would take you for his bride. That is, if your uncle could find a pig or two to trade with you." Quy laughed loudly, pleased with his joke, as he put his arm around Khai's shoulder and led him toward the well.

Loi's knees were still shaking as she trotted away. She had to hurry; the sun was already up and Má would be angry. She could hear the sounds of the nearby jungle-covered mountains—chattering monkeys, screaming parrots, and the grunts of wild pigs rooting for worms.

Loi picked up her pace until water began sloshing out all over her baggy pants. By the time she arrived at the hut, she was out of breath.

"Idle, idle girl!" Má slapped her legs with a bamboo switch. "Look, you've spilled half the water. Uncle has been ready for his tea for over ten minutes, and I had to borrow water to cook his rice. He's very angry that you've delayed him. And wipe those tears; you're not a child."

While Má quickly began preparing the tea, Loi emptied the rest of the water from the baskets into a large clay pot inside the hut. She knew what she was about to ask would make her mother even more angry, but she could not stop the question that was burning in her heart. Suddenly it blurted from her lips.

"Má, did you take money from the American soldier who was my father? I must know the truth this time."

Má's face turned as white as ashes. She grabbed her daughter by the arm and led her down the ladder and to the back where the peas and melon vines rambled up bamboo poles. Even though the woman was several inches shorter than her daughter, she was very strong.

"Never, never speak of that man again to me or in front of anyone else. As far as I am concerned, that horrible man is dead and forgotten. You must remember that if it hadn't been for your kind, generous uncle we would have starved after the war. And we would not have a home now. His life has been full of woe because he took us in. You must show more devotion and respect."

"I do respect Uncle Long and love him. But what about the American soldier? Everyone says you slept with him for money. I remember a man with yellow hair. Was he my father? What was his name? What happened to him? I need to know, Má."

"No! All you need to know is what I tell you. And I tell you to keep quiet about that American, and you will be better off. Be thankful for every scrap of food that falls into your mouth. Remember, an open mouth spills its food."

Loi knew it was pointless to speak up again. Má always refused to talk about her years in Da Nang. So Loi followed Má back into the hut. Already the aromas of tea and rice filled the air, and her young cousins were sitting around a straw mat on the floor. There wasn't much room for her, so as usual Loi slunk over to her dark corner. She could feel the children's eyes following her and knew they were pitying her. It made her sick inside.

She leaned back against the thick bamboo corner pole and listened to the click of chopsticks against rice bowls and the comments her uncle was making about the long days of hard work ahead. She hadn't eaten since late yesterday evening, but she wasn't even hungry.

Loi closed her eyes and thought of the photograph of the tall soldier with blue eyes standing next to her mother. No one knew, but Loi kept it hidden under the family altar, wrapped in a piece of the old blue *ao dai* that had belonged to her mother. In the photo, Má was holding a baby and her face was beaming with love. Whether it was love for the soldier, or for the baby, or for both, Loi guessed she would never know.

2

THE PROMISE

AFTER MORNING tea, the village women chattered like the flock of ravens that dotted the dead limbs of the old banyan tree at the edge of the fields. And the men's laughter rose as they gathered their sickles and began to discuss which field to reap first. The morning air seemed to blow new life into the villagers, and their voices crackled with anticipation of a bountiful crop.

The Lord of the Mountain and the Lord of the Sea had been merciful this year, making the rains come on schedule. In the seedbeds, thousands of tiny green rice plants had shot straight up, healthy and strong. None of the water buffaloes had gone lame while struggling to drag plows through the soggy clay paddies, and only one bull had gotten himself hurt in a fight over a bashful cow. And, miraculously, only two villagers had been bitten by water snakes while transplanting the seedlings into long, neat rows in the larger fields. All summer long the level of the irrigation ditches remained high enough for the villagers to dip their baskets and fling water to the thirsty plants. While it was true that a lone wild boar attacked and killed a woman during *lam co lua di*— the first weeding of the paddies—all in all it had been a very good season.

While Má pressed handfuls of moist rice into patties between banana leaves and Uncle Long sharpened the curved blade of the *cai liem* on a whetstone, Loi took her two youngest cousins, Hoa and Tuan, to the communal school. The children were old enough to walk the distance alone, but since the death of their mother two years earlier, they had come to expect Loi to accompany them. Besides, the schoolhouse was Loi's favorite place in the village.

The school building was the newest structure in the village, having replaced the old school that had been washed away in monsoon floods five years before. Loi still recalled families bringing baskets full of dirt to help raise the foundation. The whole village made bricks of mud and rice straw, and they cut bamboo poles for the frame and palm thatch for the roof. The school was located next to an old bomb crater that had been converted into a fish pond covered with pink lotus blooms. Some soldiers with a truckload of broken bricks and rubble from a bomb site in Nha

Trang had used the debris to build flower beds and line the jujube orchard around the school yard. Now the children tended the beds of brilliant dahlias and chrysanthemums and roses to be sold at the market-place to buy teaching supplies.

All the villagers—except the very old, the very young, and the very sick—had to help with harvest-ing, so the teacher was about the only able-bodied adult left in the village. Loi watched him command the children to form straight lines. The line that was the straightest and quietest won the honor of march-ing inside first.

Standing several meters away, Loi stared through the door at the children inside the building. Their faces were serious as they stood at attention, pledging their oath to honor their country and teacher and parents. As always, Loi's heart ached with longing to go inside and sit on one of the benches. But like so much else in her life, it was just a dream. *Con-lai* were not welcome in the schools, so Loi's mother kept her home to spare her the pain of taunting children and scowling teachers. By dim lantern light, after everyone went to sleep, Má had secretly taught Loi to read and write. And Khai had shown Loi how to do simple arithmetic.

More than anything, Loi wanted to go inside the room to learn about the places on the faded map that stretched across one wall. If she squinted and strained her eyes, she could almost distinguish the yellow shape that represented America. It didn't seem so far away from Vietnam. Just the length of a meterstick. How then could it be so different, and why then couldn't her real father come to look for her? Hadn't he left his blood flowing in her veins, just as surely as some Americans had left their blood flowing on the ground?

A chilling glance from the teacher standing in the doorway told Loi she had overstayed her welcome. She quickly returned home, where she helped Má put rice cakes into a cloth sack slung around her neck and then took the *cai liem* her uncle handed to her. As usual, it was the one with the broken handle. Má took the teapot, and they all walked in a straight line to the dike-enclosed fields, where work details had already been formed.

Loi scanned the fields of softly rippling golden grain, searching for Khai, but everyone was already bent over, their pointed leaf hats sticking out like the spikes on an overripened durian fruit.

"Get to work, idle girl," Má whispered as she rolled her baggy pants up to her knees as the others had done.

Grabbing a handful of rice stalks in her left hand, Loi slashed it *cat gat* style—halfway up—because the field was still wet and muddy from the rainy season. That meant this harvest would be far easier than the one in March, after the dry season, when she would have to cut the stalks *cat lua*—close to the ground. As they worked, a few villagers began to sing made-up songs, accompanied by the sharp crunch of blades against stalks and the soft swoosh of sheaves falling to the soggy earth. Within a very short time Loi's right hand throbbed from the pain of a raw blister where the broken handle pinched her flesh.

By noon the freshness had long vanished from the air, and the familiar sun beat down on their stooped backs. Sweat streamed down Loi's back and chest and even into her eyes because she had removed her headband to wrap her blistered hand. She vowed under her breath never to be so stupid as to leave her makeshift glove at home again.

When Loi saw the villagers breaking for the mid-day meal and ensuing nap, she sighed with relief. Some of the villagers walked back to their huts to eat and sleep, but Loi's uncle preferred to sling a woven hammock between two coconut palms that grew along the edge of the paddies, where a good breeze steadily blew.

With a body numb and stiff, Loi followed her oldest cousin, Dinh, and her Uncle Long to the shade of a large mango tree and plopped onto the soft grass. Her hand and arms throbbed with pain, and she rubbed her stiff back over and over as she waited for her mother to pour the tea.

"I guess your back aches more than mine does,

Loi," her cousin said as he unwrapped a banana leaf and bit into a ball of sticky rice. He drank some tea from a halved coconut shell.

"Why do you say that?" Loi asked. "You are working as hard as I am." Although her cousin was only twelve years old, he already had muscles as hard as stones. They often had silent races to see who could reap a row of rice the fastest. Every year he gained on her, and she feared this might be her last year to beat him.

"Well," Dinh replied, "you're so tall, you have to stoop over farther than anyone else to reach the stalks." He smiled impishly, and Loi kicked him with her bare foot. Dinh cackled with laughter and Loi's uncle joined in. His smile looked just like her mother's.

"Dinh is right. It seems to me that Loi has grown faster than a bamboo shoot since last harvest. I wonder what Officer Hiep will think when he sees that his favorite laborer is five inches taller than he is this year?"

At the mention of Officer Hiep, Loi felt a sharp lump rise to her throat, and she almost choked on her mouthful of rice.

Má removed her *non-la* and dipped her head scarf into some water.

"I don't think Officer Hiep cares about Loi's height," Má said. "She was already taller than he was last year. He's a stubborn man once he has made

28

up his mind he wants something." She patted her face and neck, trying to wash away some of the itching yellow chaff.

"I suppose we'll find out soon enough. Hiep will be arriving as soon as the rice is ready to be loaded up on the government trucks. This time, I have a feeling he is going to be talking marriage."

"No!" Loi leapt to her feet. "Uncle Long, I know I have no right to speak to you like this, and I am being very disrespectful . . . but, please, I cannot marry Officer Hiep!"

"Shhh!" Má reached up and pulled Loi back down. Loi crumpled to the ground and stared at her lap, waiting for the punishment. But her uncle held up his hand to stop Má's angry tongue.

"No, sister. Let your daughter speak. Go ahead, niece."

Loi couldn't believe her good fortune. Quickly she rose to her knees and crawled closer.

"Uncle Long, Officer Hiep is a terrible man. He's the worst possible husband in the world for me. Why, he's older than you, and every time I see him he's drinking beer or cognac or already drunk. You know he has five children from his first wife. Everyone says she died because he beat her so much. Please . . ."

Uncle Long frowned and held up his hand. Loi immediately stopped speaking and sat back on her heels.

"Enough, child. True, Officer Hiep does drink excessively and gambles too much. But what I dislike about him most is his constant boasting of his glorious feats during the revolution. To hear him talk, one would think he had been Uncle Ho's right-arm man. No one else I know carries his war medals around in his pockets."

A scowl crossed Uncle Long's face as he stared into the distance. No one dared to speak when he had that look. They had learned it meant he was thinking about the days when he was a Viet Cong soldier fighting Americans—and those of his countrymen who obeyed what he called the "puppet" southern government.

The family held its breath, wondering what he would do next. Sometimes he flew into a rage, spewing out his bitter disappointment in the leaders he had risked his life for and sacrificed members of his family for, only to end up in a small village with no land of his own. Other times he would sulk and not speak for hours, gazing off into the jungles. And once Loi had heard him crying in the middle of the night after one of his screaming nightmares. They held their breath and waited and waited.

He turned and looked straight at Loi. She knew he was thinking about her American father, wondering if it had been her father who killed his first wife and in-laws and destroyed their village. Then he blinked and pointed his finger into her face.

"Officer Hiep may not be a perfect man, but he

has a good government job and he is the *only* man who is willing to marry a fatherless *con-lai*. It will be best for you, niece. Now, no more discussion!" He stood up, shaking the rice grains from his lap. Without looking at the women, he spoke again. "Sister, make sure your daughter looks and behaves her best when Officer Hiep arrives."

"But how can she look her best when she has nothing but rags to wear? Perhaps some new cloth to make a pretty *ao dai* or a new blouse would help him overlook her shortcomings. . . ."

"Do what it takes." With that, Uncle Long walked to the hammock, slumped in it, then rolled over onto his side.

Má turned to Loi, breathless with excitement.

"See, daughter, your uncle is a kindhearted man. Now you can have a pretty new *ao dai*. I know exactly where to get some pink silk." She hugged her daughter and smiled. Loi thought her mother must have been very beautiful when she was young. In the photo she looked lovely. But now, well, it was hard to tell such things. And Má was so happy about the new cloth that Loi didn't want to say anything about Hiep right now. Maybe later. It had been so long since she had seen her mother smile like this, it was the least Loi could do not to spoil the moment, even though she didn't care about the pink silk.

After lunch, while most of the villagers were napping, Loi announced she was going for fresh drinking water. She had seen Khai across the paddies, and now she anxiously walked by him. She pretended to drop the water jug, and he picked it up for her.

"Meet me at the pool by the little waterfall. I have some terrible news," she whispered. Khai nodded.

Though her legs trembled and the blood pounded in her temples, Loi walked as calmly as she could toward the forest-covered mountains edging the paddies. She could hear the gurgling water and feel the change in temperature on her face even before she could see the stream that meandered down the mountainside. Soon she smelled the intoxicating fragrance of wild orchids and rotting leaves and damp ferns.

Loi climbed up onto a moss-covered boulder and let her bare feet dangle in the crystal-clear water that pooled up in a large basin. On the other side, sheets of foamy white water cascaded over broken boulders before tumbling into the pool. Some daring vines rambled up close to the waterfall, and some even more daring birds flitted across the stormy deluge.

A few speckled fish came to investigate her toes, then swam away, uninterested. The water was so cold it made her shiver. Or maybe it was the thought of Officer Hiep that made her shiver.

When Khai arrived, his face was cloudy and he began apologizing before Loi could speak a word.

"Loi, I'm sorry I haven't been able to work closer to you. Quy told Father about our rendezvous this morning."

"But he promised not to."

"Well, I angered him and he lost his temper. You know Quy has such hot blood. Anyway, Father ordered me to work by his side today. But he has a poor memory. I'll keep straying a little farther and soon he will have forgotten about me. Just be patient for now."

As Khai removed his black rubber thongs, made of tire scraps, Loi could hardly wait for him to stop speaking. She was about to burst with her news. When Khai climbed the boulder and sat beside her, she spoke so fast he didn't understand her at first, and Loi had to repeat herself, slowly. When her words sank in, Khai's face turned red.

"Officer Hiep! That man has the manners of a wild boar. And he struts about the village like a rooster among hens. How I despise that man." Khai turned his head aside and spat into the stream.

"Everyone does. But my uncle thinks Hiep is the only man alive who is willing to marry me because I am a *con*—" Loi suddenly stopped. She could not betray herself by forming that word on her lips. "Because of my mixed blood."

"But that isn't true. You know I want to marry you, Loi. Even more than Officer Hiep."

"But Uncle Long doesn't know that," she said softly. She could see the confusion shadowing Khai's face like dark storm clouds. "Khai . . . perhaps if you spoke to my uncle . . ."

"I cannot. I have no money to get married. I am still tending water buffaloes like a child. And my father won't give his blessing. What kind of life would we have?" Khai jerked a weed from a crevice and hurled it into the stream. Then he sighed. "At least Officer Hiep holds a position of importance and has an income. That is his one and only good trait. Perhaps . . . perhaps you would be better off with him, after all."

Loi's heart stopped beating when she heard his faltering voice. She couldn't believe these words were really coming from the lips of her darling, beloved Khai. Khai, who had pledged his eternal devotion and faithfulness; Khai, who had risked his life once to save her from an enraged buffalo and who still carried the scar on his leg like a badge of love. It was only natural for a young man to be afraid of his sweetheart's guardian. But couldn't Khai see that time was running out? Officer Hiep would be here in only a few weeks, and Loi could no longer hide her womanhood from his lusting eyes as she had managed to do in previous years.

Loi could not stand the desperation another moment. Her fingers sank into Khai's arm. She wanted to shake him like a bad child to bring him to his senses but dared not. She inhaled a deep breath, hoping to calm her voice.

"Khai, do you remember the old sacred shrine we discovered three years ago on top of this mountain?"

He nodded and a smile flickered across his lips.

"Do you recall how we pledged our love and loyalty to each other and prayed we would someday become husband and wife?"

"Yes, I remember every word we whispered. And I plucked a white orchid and put it in your hair." Khai gently brushed her hair back from her cheek. His fingers felt rough from the harvest work, but they were warm and tender. Loi's heart beat faster as she looked into his large, dark eyes. She longed to hold him close and feel his heart pounding next to hers, imagining the sound would be loud and strong, like thunder. She reached up and cupped her hand over his, drawing it closer to her face. Closing her eyes, she breathed in the dusty odor of his fingers.

"Tell me, Khai," she whispered, "was it just the idle promise children so often make and soon forget?"

Khai lifted her hand to his nose, inhaling deeply.

"No, beloved. It was not a child's promise. We saw an omen that day, sent from the spirits."

"Yes, yes." Loi felt the excitement as she recalled that special day. "It was a small wild pheasant scampering through the underbrush. A miniature replica of the celestial golden phoenix of happiness. I knew then we were destined to marry each other."

Khai gripped both her hands firmly.

"Loi, dry your eyes. I will speak to Mr. Tran and his wife tomorrow afternoon about being Matchmakers for us."

"Matchmakers!" Loi covered her mouth to stifle her shout of joy. "Oh, this is wondrous, so wondrous!" She blinked several times before she could see Khai clearly through the veil of tears. "I vow we will be happy. I will obey and honor and love you forever. . . ." The rest of the words she wanted to say lodged in her throat. Khai said nothing, but his face turned red.

As much as Loi desired to clasp him in her arms, she dared not move any closer. Other workers were coming for water, and she had stayed too long already. She quickly filled the water jug, and they parted.

When Loi returned to the harvesting, the sun didn't feel so hot on her back, nor did the work seem so harsh. She began softly humming Khai's buffalo song under her breath. Soon it would be her song—their song.

3

THE MATCH

SOMETHING WAS wrong with Loi's dream;
the screams were too loud and too close. As Loi
opened her eyes and sat up, she saw a pale light at
the front door casting grotesque shadows against the
woven straw walls of the hut. Then she heard
women's low, hushed voices. After a moment the
whispers stopped and the light bobbed across the
yard.

"Má, what's wrong?" she whispered, as her eyes
adjusted to the dark. Her mother stepped closer, holding a basket filled with rags.

"Shhh, don't wake the others. Huong is giving
birth to her baby. I am going to help."

"Shall I come with you?" Loi asked, starting to
swing her feet from the cot.

"No, stay and prepare the morning meal, and take care of the family until I return."

As her mother lit a small candle, its amber light emphasized the worried expression on the woman's smooth face.

"Má? I thought Huong's baby was not due for two more months."

"It wasn't. But something is wrong. It will be a blessing if the child lives at all."

"And what about Huong?"

Her mother pressed her lips together and turned her head away before answering.

"Go back to sleep. Today is going to be very long. You will be threshing all day."

Loi watched her mother slip out the door and silently climb down the ladder.

Loi lay on her back a moment, unable to sleep. Then she heard another scream like the one that had wrenched her from her dream. Quickly she pushed back the mosquito net and felt her way through the darkness to the family altar. She found a joss stick and lit it, then rolled it between her hands over her head. Soon the thin line of musky incense smoke curled above the photos of her deceased grandparents and great-grandparents.

Closing her eyes, Loi prayed for Huong and her baby. Although Huong was one year younger than Loi, she had already been married for a year, as had most of the other girls in the village. Some already had babies or were expecting their first very soon. Being Khai's cousin, Huong had spoken to Loi more than the other village girls had. And although she was not exactly Loi's friend, she had never been unkind.

After the prayer, Loi wanted to remove the photograph of her American father from under the altar, but she heard her cousins grumbling and shifting in their sleep, so she decided not to take the chance. She crawled back to her cot but couldn't sleep.

The sun had been up for almost two hours and Loi was beating stalks of rice against a bamboo rack. She was watching the loose yellow grains tumble into a waiting basket when her mother returned. Má seized a handful of rice sheaves and began threshing as if she were beating a disobedient dog. Like all of the women, she covered her nose and mouth with a scarf to prevent the rice dust from choking her. Soon bits of golden chaff had lodged on her cone-shaped hat and on her dark shirt. Her eyes looked red and tired, and tiny streams of water collected in their corners.

After a few minutes the two women who had been at Loi's door that morning joined the threshing and began whispering to the other threshers. Loi expected her mother to speak, but she remained silent, beating the sheaves over and over, until a cloud of golden dust whirled in the air above her head.

When they took a break later that morning, Loi handed her mother some cold rice and a coconut shell filled with water.

"Má? Is Huong's baby all right?"

"The child was born dead."

Loi bit her lip and turned her head away for a moment as tears moistened her eyes.

"And Huong? Is she all right?"

"She is alive." Loi's mother finished her drink and handed the empty shell back to her daughter.

"Poor Huong. Was the child a boy or a girl?"

"It was neither . . . and it was both."

Loi raised her hand to cover her gasp.

"Another child like . . . like the others? But Huong is so careful. She never drinks milk from the coconuts that come from the south. And she never walks across the barren spot on the other side of the mountain. She is the most cautious girl I've ever known. How . . . ?"

"It was her husband. He was raised in another province. Who knows what he may have eaten or where he may have walked. We warned Huong's mother not to allow the marriage. We all saw the boy's thumb."

Suddenly Loi remembered Huong's husband. He was handsome and strong, with only one visible flaw: his left thumb was twice the normal size and had two distinct nails, as if two thumbs had sprouted out of the same joint. It had seemed so unimportant.

A shiver ran through Loi's body. This was the third malformed baby born in their village. But the others had been born to girls who were careless, who dared to eat coconuts and fruits from poisoned provinces or who strolled on the other side of the mountain. Uncle Long said the jungle there had once been as thick and lush as the others, and full of parrots and monkeys, before the American airplanes dumped their death clouds. Now, even after twenty years, nothing grew among the black skeletons of trees except scrubby vines and a few saplings.

Loi's mother remained silent the rest of the day, threshing with an intensity that didn't seem normal. When the others assembled to leave, Loi's mother showed no sign of quitting and the women ignored her. After they had walked away, she laid down her handful of stalks and crumpled to the ground in exhaustion. She tugged the scarf free from her face and breathed deeply.

"What happened to your face and neck, Má?" Loi asked.

"Just some scratches." The woman brushed Loi away and reached for the water jug.

"Was it Huong who scratched you? She was screaming so much."

All the while Loi's mother poured water on her scarf and wiped her face and neck, her eyes remained on the single file of women crossing the bamboo bridge over the irrigation ditch.

"It doesn't matter who scratched me. Everyone in the room felt Huong's pain. People in pain slash out the same way as a wounded animal. I cannot blame her."

As her mother rose and shook off the loose chaff, Loi knew it was pointless to question her further. But that night her uncle and her mother argued loudly, and Loi knew the fight centered on her American father. Huong's mother was the one who had scratched Má, because the Americans had brought the poison to the jungles. And since Loi's mother had slept with an American, she would have to bear the anger of the village. And so would Loi.

For days the only thing the village women spoke about was Huong's malformed baby. Some claimed it had had two heads; others swore that it had had a head growing from its stomach and three sets of limbs. Loi felt sorry for Huong, who had always had a sweet smile on her round face. She tried to visit Huong several times, but the girl's family chased Loi away, and Huong refused to come out of her hut. Several girls said that Huong would never be able to have any more children because her womb had been damaged.

One week later, Loi's mother announced over the morning rice that Huong was dead. The unhappy girl had taken her own life by jumping into the village well.

—

Although Loi felt deep sorrow for Huong's tragedy, she could not help but think about her own future with Khai. At first she was not overly concerned when the Matchmakers did not approach her uncle's hut. After all, Huong had been Khai's cousin, and surely it was out of respect for her misfortune that Khai was delaying the marriage arrangements. But now weeks had passed and the harvest work was in its final stages. The threshing had been completed and the baskets of rice, still in their yellow husks, had been spread out on the road or on straw mats to dry in the sun. Every day, boys shuffled through the rice, turning the grains over with their bare feet or with a wooden rake. After the drying, the grains would be tossed into the air to separate the hulls from the rice. The best grains would become *lua giong*, seed for next season's crop, while the bad darkened rice—*lua lep*—was discarded. Rumors buzzed through the village that already government trucks were rumbling in the villages to the south, which were always harvested earlier than theirs.

"Please let the Matchmakers come," Loi prayed each night before she slept and each morning before she started her work. But still they did not come. And worse than this, Khai did not speak to her. At first she was sure it was because of his cousin's tragedy and his shyness, but several times she saw him with his water buffalo preparing next season's seedbed, and he turned his head away. But far worse, he no longer sang their special song of love.

The afternoon shadows were growing long as Loi pounded a bowl of rice with a pestle to separate the bran from the kernels, and then sieved out the broken rice pieces for chicken feed. She poured the last of the clean white rice into a large basket and raked her arm across her sweaty brow. The bran and dust stuck to her body and itched like the bites of an army of hungry mosquitoes. Loi's legs shook with weariness, but she knew what she would do next. The pool of cool, clean water from the mountain stream was beckoning her, as it did every day at this time. It was growing late, but Loi knew she would not be able to sleep until she had cleansed off the biting pieces of rice hulls and layers of dirt and dust.

Although Loi ached all over, as she walked down the forest path leading to the pool, she began to feel the great sense of relief that always came after a day of hard work, and especially after the end of the harvest. For a while at least, the village women would be able to relax before planting the next crop, which would be harvested in the spring. Of course, there still remained the chore of gathering vegetables from her mother's garden and taking them to market in a nearby town. That in itself was the closest thing to a vacation any villager ever had.

At the pool, Loi removed her clothes and washed them, then she wrung them out and laid them on the moss-covered rock ledge overhanging the basin. The air was still hot enough that within an hour they would be dry.

Huge chill-bumps rose to Loi's skin as her toes first touched the cold water. But soon she adjusted to it and dove in head first. She swam underwater, holding her breath until she saw the ripples beneath the waterfall. When she came up, the water pounded her head like a drum. She laughed and dove in again and again, finding renewed strength in the refreshing water. She practiced swimming on her stomach and on her back until the evening shadows grew long across the rock ledge.

Loi climbed out of the pool and touched her clothes. They were still damp, but dry enough to wear. By the time she walked to her hut, they would be completely dry. A songbird warbled out a happy tune, and Loi was overcome with the desire to feel the cool water again. She poised on the moss-covered rock for one final dive, breathing in the sweet fragrance of wild orchids and ferns and watching a flash of blue as birds dashed recklessly across the waterfall. She remembered the last time she had seen Khai standing on this very rock. His touch had been so warm and his words so sincere. Suddenly she was filled with courage and vowed silently that she would speak to him first thing in the morning, when he drove the buffaloes to pasture.

Taking a deep breath, Loi plunged into the pool

and came up on the far side, shaking the beads of water from her face. The sound of deep, rollicking laughter echoed off the rock walls and burst into Loi's peaceful world. She spun around and looked up at the ledge. A man wearing a khaki-colored military uniform with red epaulettes and knee-high boots bowed low as he swept his cap off his head. Thick black hair, speckled with gray at the temples, tumbled into his piercing dark eyes.

"My compliments on your diving and swimming, Miss Loi. You're as talented as a river otter but many times more lovely."

Loi sank deeper into the water, so that only her nose and eyes peeked out. She watched the short, muscular man squat on the rock, scoop his cap full of water, and take a long, noisy drink. Then he laughed again, showing large teeth, yellowed from a lifetime of smoking tobacco.

"I knew you were turning into a beauty, but my eyes can hardly believe what they see. Last year you were just a delicate pink bud; now you're a fully ripened lotus blossom ready to be picked. Come up here where I can see you better." He patted the rock.

Loi shook her head and back-paddled until she was almost at the waterfall. She could barely hear his words above the roar of the water pelting her head and shoulders. But there was no mistaking the man's lusty grin and the look in his eyes.

"Very well. Timidity is a virtue among women.

But how are you going to get home without these?"
He grabbed her clothes and held them out above the
pool. When Loi didn't move, he shook his head and
made a clicking noise with his tongue.

"Such a shame your clothes are so ragged. If you
were my wife, you would be wearing fresh, clean
clothes every day. Come get these before I drop them
in the water. A pity. They're almost dry." He
dangled the clothes and shook them, while his dark
eyes strained to see her body through the water. Still
holding her clothes, he climbed down from the rock
and started around the pool. Loi sank under the water
and swam to the opposite side. When she came up
she saw him standing on a ledge.

"Come, come. I don't have time for games. You'll
be in a fine mess if you have to return to the village
naked." His eyes narrowed and his mouth became a
tight, thin line. Loi remained silent as she watched
him pace a few times, then curse under his breath.
Suddenly he wadded the clothes into a ball and threw
them into the water with all his might. A whirlpool
caught them and slowly pulled them under. Then he
put one hand on his hip and pointed the other at Loi.

"You'd better learn to obey, if you're going to be
the wife of an important officer like me. I don't mind
friskiness in a young woman, but disobedience will
not be tolerated. I'll be seeing you again very soon,
my pretty pink lotus." With that he turned on his
boot heels and leapt off the ledge, landing lightly on

his feet before crashing down the trail, slapping tree limbs out of his way and cursing out loud.

Loi let out her breath and waited several minutes until she was sure he was gone. Then she quickly pulled her soaked clothes out of the stream, where they had lodged against a boulder. She wrung them as dry as possible, then dressed and ran toward the village.

As she paused at the top of the ladder to catch her breath, she heard unfamiliar voices—a man's and a woman's—coming from inside the hut. Slowly creeping to the door, she peered around the opening and waited for her eyes to adjust to the darkness inside. She drew in her breath in a sharp gasp and put her hands over her mouth to stifle the cry.

"The Matchmakers!" she whispered and hugged her body. "At last! Oh, thank the gods and thank you, honored ancestors, for finally granting my wish. Khai has certainly taken his time making arrangements, but it doesn't matter. All that matters is I will be free from Officer Hiep and his lustful eyes. Oh, thank you, good, gentle Khai."

Loi closed her eyes and gave a silent prayer of thanks to her ancestors. She ran her fingers through her wet hair and tried to straighten her clothes as best she could, while thinking of what she would say. She didn't want to look unpresentable to the Matchmakers.

Loi smiled and breathed deeply. But as she took

her first step forward, the ladder shook from the weight of someone climbing up. Before Loi could turn around, a strong hand grabbed her shoulder and pushed her inside the hut. Stumbling forward, Loi fell to her knees in front of the startled Matchmakers and her uncle.

"I've found my reluctant bride," a man's voice boomed. Loi didn't bother to look up. She knew the tone and boisterous laugh all too well.

"Officer Hiep, please come in," Loi's uncle said, rushing across the room. "I was just listening to the offer the Matchmakers were proposing on your behalf. A marriage between you and my sister's daughter is my greatest dream. Welcome."

Loi felt a wave of nausea sweep over her body as she swooned and reeled forward.

4

THE ENGAGEMENT

WHEN LOI awakened, the hut was dark and silent. Through the opening in the woven mat wall, she could see the stars of the dragon constellation hanging low in the sky and knew she had been sleeping for several hours. A deep, gnawing hunger reminded Loi that she hadn't eaten since lunchtime yesterday, and as she crawled to her feet, her stiff, aching muscles reminded her of the strenuous work of the past weeks. She felt her way to the three-legged stove and the pole where a sack of rice was hanging. Rats scampered away, but Loi was not interested in chasing them. She ate a handful of raw rice grains, then left the hut and walked to the cultivated area surrounded by a fence of tall living bamboo.

In her mother's vegetable garden, she plucked a ripe tomato, wiped off the heavy dew, then devoured it. The time was fast approaching for them to gather all the vegetables and take them to market. It was her mother's favorite time of year because the garden was hers and hers alone. The men did not lift a finger to work in it. And unlike the rice, which had to be shared with the government authorities, the profits from the vegetables belonged solely to Má.

Loi dug up a carrot and ate half of it. She put the rest into her pants pocket for later. There would still be a couple of hours before the rest of the village woke up. It would be a simple matter to dig up some vegetables, put them in a sack, and run away. She knew the way to the main highway that led to Da Lat, and from there she could catch a bus to any place she wanted.

Loi's brain swam with a million details of what to do. She sighed. A life alone—without her family or Khai—would be worse than what she had now. And once she ran away, she would never be able to face them again. Besides, she did not know for sure that the Matchmakers had made a marriage arrangement. After all, Uncle Long hated Officer Hiep as much as she did.

"What are you doing out here, child?"

Loi leapt to her feet. "Má! I . . . I was hungry, so I ate a tomato."

"Tst, tst. You mustn't eat all my profits away." She turned the tomato vines over and began picking the ripest ones.

"What are you doing up so early, Má?"

"I thought I heard rabbits in my garden. But it was only you—the biggest kind of rabbit I've ever seen." She smiled slightly. Loi couldn't remember the last time her mother had teased her, although she often played such games with the smaller children. And she didn't seem to be angry about the tomato. Loi squatted down beside her and began helping pull up a few long white radishes. Loi cleared her throat.

"Má? Did the Matchmakers make an arrangement?"

"Yes, indeed. The engagement party will be in one week."

"One week!" Loi stood up. "Why so soon?"

"Officer Hiep is an impatient man, and he is also practical. He wants to have the engagement party when he returns to collect the rice quota, so he won't have to make an extra trip down here."

"But Uncle Long hates Officer Hiep. How could he have agreed?"

"He hasn't agreed yet, you know that. There is still the engagement party. If Hiep's gifts are unsuitable, there will not be a wedding."

Loi sighed and snapped a radish in two. "I suppose his gifts will be wonderful, though."

"I've heard he is a rich man. You should be grateful for this marriage. Many other girls would be pleased."

"I don't care about his wealth! I would rather be married to a wild boar in the woods." Loi looked at the scowl that formed on her mother's face, then she turned and walked away.

Lying in bed, Loi felt tears slide out of the corners of her eyes as she stared up at the ceiling. She heard the first rooster call out his challenge, then a chorus of replies all over the village. Then came the sound Loi had been waiting for—the low bellow of a water buffalo and the voices of the singing boys.

She leapt from her straw mat, climbed down the ladder, and waited near the trail that led to the pastures. She strained her eyes until she recognized the outline of Khai, sitting tall and straight on top of the lead bull.

"Khai!" she whispered and began walking alongside the giant black animal. "I must talk to you."

"What is wrong?"

"Officer Hiep was here yesterday."

"I know. I saw his motorcycle."

"And the Matchmakers were at my uncle's hut yesterday."

"Oh . . ." Khai's voice trailed off as he slid from the water buffalo. "Loi, I tried. I tried over and over, but . . ."

"But what? You promised me you would talk to the Matchmakers. That was almost a month ago. I waited and waited, giving you every excuse possible. I said nothing when you turned your face from me. But now . . . now it's too late. The engagement party is in one week, and I am doomed to live with that . . . that swine for the rest of my life. I hope you are happy with whomever your brother and father select for *you* to marry. At least one of us might lead a normal life." Loi swung around to hide the wave of bitter tears that flowed from her eyes, but her body began to shake uncontrollably.

"Loi, you mustn't hate me. I did try. Again and again. I asked three different couples to be the Matchmakers. Each time, the women refused, saying they could not arrange such a marriage. They said it was too dishonorable for them."

Slowly Loi turned back around and saw that Khai's eyes flamed with anger.

"They all refused?"

"Yes. All of the stupid old crows. I didn't want to tell you. I was waiting for the proper moment to explain. Then my cousin Huong's misfortune happened. I was going to tell you soon but . . ."

Loi held her breath, then expelled it slowly. "I suppose the silly old women thought they were protecting you because they didn't think I would be a proper wife."

Khai jerked a piece of cane from the earth and snapped it in two. "I begged and pleaded with them. I even considered going to your uncle without a Matchmaker."

"Isn't it strange that the Matchmakers think I'm

not good enough for you, but they think I'm perfect for Officer Hiep."

"It's his perfect money they love. Hiep thinks he can buy anything or anyone with money. How I despise that pig! I can't believe your uncle is throwing you to a drunkard like that. If anything happens to you, I'll never forgive your Uncle Long. . . ."

"No, Khai, it's not Uncle Long's fault. He's only doing what he thinks is best for me. I know he hates Officer Hiep. It's the Matchmakers who are so anxious to get me out of the village forever. I understand their scheme very well." Loi stared across the fields toward the village. The swirling mists formed eerie halos around each lantern-lit hut. And then she saw the outline of the village well. All her life she had heard stories about troubled girls ending their problems at the bottom of that well.

"I think I know the answer," she whispered, more to herself than to Khai, and began walking in slow, determined steps toward the well. It seemed to beckon her through the mists, and all the lost souls of its victims seemed to hold out their hands toward her like loving sisters.

She reached the stone rim of the well and stared down at its darkness. She saw the faces of the famous Trung sisters, who threw themselves into a raging river when the Chinese defeated their army in battle; then the angry face of the young woman general Trieu Au, who fell on her own sword rather than admit defeat. Then she saw the sad, plump face of Huong. Never before had Loi noticed how black and bottomless and cold the well appeared. A shiver shook her frame.

Suddenly she felt Khai's warm hands on her cold skin. He pulled her close and cradled her tenderly against his chest as he spoke softly.

"Throwing yourself into the well is no answer. What would I do without you to encourage me all the time? You are my beautiful mountain fairy, remember?" He cupped her face in his hands and wiped her tears with his thumbs.

"But there is no other way." Loi sighed. "It is the only honorable thing to do. Then perhaps my mother and uncle will understand how horrible this marriage arrangement truly is."

"No, no, no. Do not think of taking your life. Besides, knowing Officer Hiep, he would hold your Uncle Long responsible for your death and send him to reeducation camp. We must think of another way. We must." Khai sat on the edge of the well and propped his chin in his hands.

"Well, a thought did occur to me last night. If somehow I had an accident and was mutilated or became a cripple, perhaps Hiep wouldn't have such desire for me. But then . . . maybe you wouldn't, either. . . ."

Khai shook his head at first, then a strange light appeared in his eyes. He jumped to his feet.

"Loi, you've given me an idea. I heard my grandmother tell a story once. An engagement was arranged for a young girl in her village by the Matchmakers, but the prospective husband was very old and ugly. The girl loved a young man who had no money."

"This story sounds all too familiar. But go on, what happened?"

"According to the tale, the girl decided to make herself so undesirable that the old man would not want to marry her. At the party, although she was an excellent cook, she ruined the food. She wore the most raggedy and ugly clothes and stuffed her *ao dai* with straw to make her back look humped. She painted red spots all over her face to make herself look diseased. Then she spoke to him with a terrible stutter and slurred her words like an imbecile."

Loi broke into laughter as she pictured the scene.

"Well, did it work?"

"Most certainly. The old man called off the engagement. Unfortunately, the girl developed such a bad reputation that no one wanted to marry her after that, not even the poor young man. She died a childless, bitter old maid with no one to look after her grave."

"I'm willing to take that chance. Oh, Khai, thank you for the wonderful idea. I will be so ugly and undesirable that even Officer Hiep's hot, lustful blood will turn cold."

"But you must be prepared for your uncle's wrath. You must tell him it was my idea if he tries to strike you."

"I will stuff my pants with straw so his beating won't be so painful. It will be worth it."

After that morning Loi did not mention her engagement again. She performed her duties diligently and helped her mother in the garden every day like a model daughter. But as she pulled weeds and hauled baskets of water and chased off rabbits and blackbirds, she carefully planned what she would do. And she secretly collected everything she would need: a handful of rice flour, a red beet, some poisonous weeds, some straw, and some bitter roots.

The night before the party, Loi's mother adjusted the lantern light and hunched over a piece of pink silk. Her delicate brown fingers flew over the cloth as they pulled yellow thread into an intricate design. The silk came from an old woman in the village who had once seen better times but was now forced to sell off her possessions one by one. The pink material had once been a lovely *ao dai* that the old woman had worn in Hue the day she watched Emperor Bao Dai riding inside a palanquin outside the Forbidden Purple City citadel. Loi's mother had carefully recut the silk to fit Loi's body and embroidered a golden phoenix on the front panel. The pants to accompany it—long, billowy white ones—were borrowed from a neighbor.

Loi busied herself in the cooking area, preparing special dishes for the party. When no one was looking, she set aside a few ingredients for *cha gio*, the small meat rolls she normally cooked so well. Tomorrow she would add some crushed bitter roots to a few of them. The pork would be rotten and the mushrooms moldy, to ensure that they would taste terrible. These were for Officer Hiep, and she would serve them herself in her rags and spotted face.

A little later, Loi's mother slipped the *ao dai* around Loi's body and began fastening the hooks under her arms. It fit her perfectly, accentuating her high, small bust and narrow waist. Each separate panel cascaded gracefully to just below her knees, revealing the white pants along the unfastened sides and the bottom.

Loi slid her fingers over the cool, shimmery cloth. Never in her life had Loi possessed such a beautiful garment. In her heart she wanted to twirl around and prance in front of everyone, especially Khai. But she would not allow herself to think about such vanity. By the time of the party tomorrow, the dress would be far from beautiful.

Loi's mother squatted and rocked back on her heels as she tugged at the front panel. The lantern light turned her skin a soft amber.

"You are the most beautiful angel in this village. No matter what the others say," she whispered as her dark eyes grew larger.

Loi was surprised to hear her mother speaking so kindly.

"I only wish I had some real golden thread, and silk that wasn't so old and faded. You must be very careful. This cloth is so rotten it will rip at the slightest strain. And look how crooked this poor phoenix is. I didn't have enough thread, I'm afraid."

"It's fine, Má."

"When I was a girl, it was my dream to have a pink *ao dai* with a golden phoenix on the front panel. I dreamed of it often and imagined who would attend my engagement party and what expensive gifts of gold jewelry I would receive. And for my wedding, a red silk *ao dai* with great golden peonies on it. My mother had purchased the cloth when I was only fourteen because she had seen it in a shop in Hue one day and fell in love with it. My mother was always doing things like that, always thinking of my future engagement party and wedding. I suppose it was because she had only one daughter, and she wanted my life to be special."

Loi looked down at her mother's dark eyes staring across the room in a trance, communicating with the imaginary ghosts of relatives long dead. In the soft lantern light, Loi could almost visualize her mother's youthful beauty.

"Did you know that when I was fifteen," Má spoke to the night, "three young suitors asked Matchmakers to speak to my father? But my mother didn't like any of them. They were not good enough for me, she said, and I was too young to marry. She talked my father out of listening to them. She had her eye on the son of an old, respectable mandarin family. Oh, that one was so very handsome. And arrogant as a cobra, with his black eyes and haughty head held up straight and tall."

Loi's mother rose, crossed the room, and took down a *non-la* from a peg. But this cone-shaped hat wasn't plain like the ones the farmers wore. Uncle Long had brought this one all the way from Hue, and it had beautiful etchings on its side. When she held it up to the light, a scene of two girls walking over a bridge appeared. Loi's mother shifted the hat until the light gleamed on the scene, then she traced the outline with her fingertips.

"The first time I saw him it was spring and the moats around the citadel were choked with pink lotus blossoms. He was crossing over the River of Perfumes, walking beside his old father. That old white-bearded man was in his blue-and-gold mandarin's *ao dai* and scholar's cap, even though the emperor had abdicated many years before. I had never seen a more handsome or grand young man in my life. I was so engrossed I dropped my new silk umbrella into the moat, and my mother was too embarrassed for words.

I had to kneel before the altar an hour that afternoon as punishment."

Loi removed the engagement dress and gently folded it. Her mother was in a strange mood indeed, talking about things so long ago. If she had been so popular and lovely, why hadn't she married that mandarin's son? If she had, Loi would never have been born and would not be in such a miserable dilemma now about having to marry an old, repulsive man like Officer Hiep. Loi waited for her mother to finish the story, though she really didn't care. Obviously her mother had not married the handsome young man, and besides, Loi's own problems demanded all her attention. After a long silence, she finally spoke.

"So, what happened to the mandarin's handsome, arrogant son?"

The woman blinked and lowered the *non-la* from the light.

"Why . . . I don't know. The Northern Army soldiers took all of his family away and none of them came back. It was New Year's time, the year our lovely home in Hue was destroyed by bombs and my family moved to Da Nang. After that, it didn't matter what kind of dress I wore for my wedding."

Loi's mother returned the hat to its peg, and when she came back her eyes were hard and her lips tight. Without warning, she was back to normal, snapping commands to Loi and criticizing her for not preparing the green mung-bean pudding correctly. Loi sighed as she stepped aside to get out of the short woman's path. Maybe it was better for her mother to be this way. Then, at least, Loi wouldn't have to feel guilty about ruining the pink *ao dai*.

Later that night, after her mother had cleaned the family altar and set out fresh fruit and flowers and blown out the last candle, Loi lay on her cot unable to sleep. She was startled to find her mother standing over her, straightening the mosquito net and fussing over the engagement gown again.

"Má, . . . that mandarin's son you told me about—," Loi whispered. "You loved him, didn't you?"

"Love? Oh, don't be silly, child. How can you love someone you've never met or even spoken to?"

"But you knew what he looked like, and where he lived, and about his family, didn't you?"

"I had seen him from afar, that's all."

"But it must have been love. You preferred him over the others who proposed, didn't you?"

Má kneeled beside Loi's mat and slipped her hand over her daughter's. Her whisper, though low and soft, seemed to fill the entire hut.

"I was young and frivolous, a mere girl of fifteen. I knew nothing of life. My head was full of foolish dreams of red wedding gowns and long life and a handsome husband. All girls have such dreams. But the truth is that you must marry the man chosen for you. You bear his children and live your life as best you can. If you are very lucky indeed, your children will be healthy and take care of you in your old age, and your husband will not beat you. That is all. Now go to sleep. I want you to be rested and lovely tomorrow."

"Má, why didn't you return to Hue after the war? It sounds like a pretty city."

"It was the most beautiful city on earth. But after Da Nang, I could not. . . . I was *chua hoang*—an unwed mother."

"Surely we have family there. Maybe someone would marry you now."

"No! After Da Nang I had nothing. Of all my brothers, only your Uncle Long would forgive me, and he is still paying the price for that kindness. Now, sleep."

Loi heard her mother whispering in front of the altar and then the soft sobs she had heard so many nights before. Loi rolled onto her side and stared at the bright stars twinkling through the opening. She thought she would like to cry, too, but her eyes remained dry as she clenched her teeth and swore under her breath she would never be like her mother, who accepted what other men willed. If the American blood coursing through her veins made her so different in the eyes of the world, then, by heaven! she would act differently. She would marry Khai, no matter what the price.

5

THE ARGUMENT

LOI STARED out her window at the troupe of
people walking down the road, led by the Matchmakers. She studied the old, gray-haired woman on Officer Hiep's arm, then sighed. Loi had known they
would arrive at the designated time, yet her heart had
not given up hope until this moment. Soon she heard
the shuffle of people removing their sandals and the
high-pitched voice of Mrs. Matchmaker asking permission to bring the groom and his family inside.

With legs of lead, Loi lifted herself from her cot
and joined her family at the door. The party of guests
waiting inside was small. Loi's mother had few close
friends and no relatives in the village. For this, Loi
was glad. The fewer people who saw her misery, the
better.

Before letting the groom's party enter, Loi's mother quickly examined her daughter one more time, then smiled her approval. The pink *ao dai* hugged Loi's slender waist and small breasts and flowed gracefully to her knees in two separate panels. The white silk pants billowed to the floor, making Loi seem to float when she took small, dainty steps like her mother's.

Because he lived so far away, Hiep had brought only a few relatives with him—a cousin in an army uniform, a brother and his wife, and his old mother, whose black eyes scrutinized the inside of the hut as she stepped over the threshold. When her black gaze fell on Loi, a grunt of displeasure erupted from her lips and she quickly whispered something into her older son's ear. Loi felt her body melting into a puddle of humiliation. Living with Hiep and raising his five children would be bad enough, but living with a severe mother-in-law would be no less than slavery.

Two village women brought in a tray of rice wine and a tray of three lime-coated betel leaves wrapped around areca palm nuts. After introducing the family members, Mrs. Matchmaker presented each of the mothers with one of the betel leaves and kept the third for herself. Mr. Matchmaker, a meek, balding man, gave rice wine to Loi's uncle and to Hiep's older brother.

There were very few gifts from friends in the village, just two candlesticks from Má's closest friend and two vases from Uncle Long's best friend. But Loi didn't mind. She didn't want the villagers to waste their money on gifts for a marriage that was doomed from the start. Hiep had not even allowed the astrologers to consult the charts to choose a proper engagement date. He chose it himself, for his own convenience—a sure sign of terrible luck.

Loi could tell that Hiep did not care about the engagement formalities. After all, this was his second wife, and many men in his situation dismissed the engagement ceremony altogether. Loi watched Hiep impatiently receive the gifts, then walk to the door, where he had left a large basket. He lifted out a tray covered with a long silk scarf.

Loi's mother and the guests gasped as he lifted the scarf to reveal flashing gold jewelry and a stack of money. Loi's heart sank farther. Now there was no chance that her mother or uncle would cancel the engagement. Even Loi could hardly take her eyes off the beautiful gold bracelets, neck chains, and earrings. And, of course, the money was more than enough to pay for the engagement party.

Finally the moment arrived that Loi had dreaded the most. Officer Hiep took her hand and they bowed low before the ancestral altar, while Mr. Matchmaker declared them officially engaged. Loi felt Hiep's hand squeeze hers fiercely, but she jerked it free and followed her mother and Hiep's mother into a little room in the back of the hut that had been sectioned off with a bamboo screen. The older woman's eyes bore first into Loi's mother, then into Loi, as she slipped the gold jewelry onto her withered old arms and neck. As was the custom, she would wear the jewelry until the party was over.

"My son certainly has good taste in jewelry," she said. "These jewels are far better than the ones he gave to that first wife of his. She was nothing but a trollop. I told him that from the start. She was useless around the house and couldn't stand up to a day's work. I never saw such a disobedient, willful girl. She had to be beaten nearly every week. I hope my foolish son has learned his lesson and has chosen better this time." Her tiny eyes pierced into Loi as she spoke.

"My daughter will make an excellent wife," Loi's mother said in a strong voice. "She's intelligent and knows how to cook far better than other girls her age. And she works like a buffalo. She's never even been sick."

Loi wanted to vomit. How could her mother grovel before that old woman and peddle her own daughter as if she were no more than a piglet in the marketplace? Loi felt her stomach grow tight, and breathing became more difficult. She wanted to stand up and scream, to run out the door and never come back, no matter what the consequences. Starvation, poverty, pain—nothing could be as horrible as life with Hiep and this old hag.

Hiep's mother grunted her doubts, then returned to the rest of the guests, parading the gold jewelry and bragging about her precious son.

"Don't worry, daughter," Loi's mother whispered as they reentered the main room, "she won't live much longer."

For the final time, Loi and Hiep bowed in front of the altar. Then he slipped a simple gold ring onto her finger, and she gave him the ring her Uncle Long had purchased. As soon as the deed was done, a cheer rose up and the guests began laughing and devouring the feast spread out on the floor—barbecued red pork, meat rolls, sweet rice cakes, fresh fruit, tea for the women, and wine and beer for the men.

With her legs still shaking, Loi excused herself and vanished into the screened-off room. For a moment, she slumped to the floor and allowed her body to shake with sobs. Then she pawed at the tears and clenched her teeth as she prepared herself for her last hope.

She arranged the special *cha gio* she had made with spoiled pork on a tray, then pulled out the items she had been collecting all week. She carefully powdered her face and hands with flour until her skin took on a ghostly white pallor. Then she dotted her smooth skin with patches of red beet juice. With trembling fingers, she splattered grease and dirt on the front panel of her *ao dai* and ripped its seams. She loosened her intricately knotted hair her mother had worked so hard to weave, and let her curls hang loose.

Loi prayed to her ancestors for courage, then scooped up the tray and walked toward Officer Hiep. He and the other men sat in the middle of the room, circled around a mat covered with food and drink. The women ate in the back near the kitchen, supervising the cooking and hustling to keep the men's glasses filled.

Loi stopped in front of Officer Hiep.

"I've prepared these delicacies especially for you, Officer Hiep. They are the best I've ever made," she said, keeping her eyes downcast as she laid the tray at his feet.

He looked up, smiling, but when he saw her face, his smile disappeared.

"Child, what's wrong with your face? Are you sick?" He scooted away, as if to avoid breathing her air.

"Yes. I-I do feel terribly ill. I think I've caught some awful disease."

"What disease?" Her uncle leapt up, grabbed Loi's arm, and led her out the door into the sunlight. Uncle Long forced her chin up and ran his finger across her cheek, leaving a swath of clean skin in the middle of the white flour.

"What kind of foolishness are you up to?" He hissed. "Clean your face and change those soiled clothes. Do you want to make Officer Hiep change his mind and call off the engagement?"

"Nothing would make me happier, Uncle Long. I hate Officer Hiep! I would rather die than marry him."

"Insolent girl! You'd be lucky if a mountain savage wanted to marry someone who acts like you." He shook her arm as he dragged her toward the bamboo screen. "Make yourself presentable and apologize to Hiep and his family."

Loi stumbled to the floor from the force of his shove and tasted blood in the corner of her mouth. In a moment her mother's firm hands were washing her face, combing her hair, and removing the soiled *ao dai*. When the woman saw the stains and rips, a little cry came from her lips, but she said nothing. In a few moments she led Loi back to the main room, where Hiep and his mother were arguing violently, while the rest of the party stood in stunned silence.

"She's the most spiteful, undisciplined girl I have ever seen. Never in all my years have I seen a girl so willful at her own engagement party. It's unheard of. Only a child that has the blood of a foreigner in her would be so insolent! I won't have her in my house! I won't have her!" The woman's shrill voice cut into the air like the edge of a dagger, but Hiep put his arms around his mother and drew her aside, speaking in low, persuasive tones for several minutes. Finally he hugged her and she walked to a corner, where she sat beside her oldest son and his pale wife.

Loi's mother forced her daughter toward the seated family.

"Mrs. Truong," she said, bowing low, "my daughter wishes to apologize to you and your family for her childish, disrespectful behavior." Her nails dug deeply into Loi's arm.

"I regret the embarrassment I have caused," Loi muttered. The old woman grunted and Hiep's brother said it didn't matter. His thin wife looked at Loi with large, frightened eyes as if she wanted to speak, but quickly changed her mind and dropped her gaze to the floor.

Loi repeated her apology to Officer Hiep, then to her Uncle Long. A few moments later the men were lifting their glasses in a toast and laughing as if nothing had happened. When Hiep tasted Loi's special meat rolls, he grimaced slightly but ate them without complaint.

Loi's mother refused to speak to her and turned her back any time her daughter came near. Hiep's family remained aloof and separate from the rest of the party, and they were the first of the guests to leave. By this time, the men had emptied several jugs of homemade rice wine, a bottle of French cognac, and many cans of beer that Hiep had brought from the city.

Soon it grew dark outside, and Loi's youngest two

cousins and her mother retired to the sleeping area. Loi remained in the kitchen, cleaning dishes and waiting on the few men who remained drinking with Officer Hiep and her Uncle Long. The more Hiep drank, the looser his tongue and hands became. Every time Loi brought out more food or drink, he tried to pull her to his side. And each time Loi pushed him away and turned her face from his foul breath, he roared with laughter.

Loi's legs ached from standing so long, and she sighed with gratitude when the last of the men staggered out the door. But her greatest wish, that Hiep be gone with them, was not granted. He remained seated on the floor beside the dirty plates and beer cans scattered on the mat. Across from him, Uncle Long still sat cross-legged. Now they were arguing and gesturing, each one trying to outshout the other.

"Why do drunken men always think no one can hear their voices?" Dinh asked as Loi lowered her weary body to the floor and leaned against the corner pole.

"Perhaps their ears are so full of wine they cannot hear their own voices," Loi suggested and smiled weakly.

"That was a wild trick you tried to play on Hiep today. But I don't think it worked. He seems as anxious as ever to marry you."

Loi nodded and closed her eyes. "I'll think of something else. There must be something that will make Hiep not want to marry me. You know, I put rotten pork and bitter roots in the *cha gio*, and Hiep ate them anyway."

"His tongue was probably too numb from wine to taste anything."

"What do you think I should try next?"

"You may not have to worry about trying any more tricks. Hiep may not marry you after all. Look."

"What?" Loi opened her eyes.

Dinh nodded in the direction of the two men, whose arguing had climbed to a crescendo. Suddenly Loi's uncle rose to his feet and pointed an accusing finger toward the short, muscular man in the brown uniform.

"I'm tired of hearing about you and the glorious revolution," he shouted. "I'm sick of hearing about the Party's great achievements. The Party did this, the Party did that, the Party's latest goals . . . This is what the Party has done for me."

Loi's uncle jerked his shirt off, tearing a sleeve in his eagerness to reveal the large red scar that extended from his right shoulder all the way down his rib cage and vanished into the top of his trousers.

"You are not the only soldier who was wounded in the war. How many millions lost their lives?" Hiep drained the cup in front of him, then tossed it across the room.

"Don't speak to me of death!" Loi's uncle shouted. "I watched my beautiful first wife and her family—her parents and younger sisters—killed. I wept, but I kept that memory inside me each time I crawled through the mud, my blood drained by leeches, my body devoured by mosquitoes and shivering from malaria. Sometimes I only had a few grains of raw rice to eat. We dared not light a fire to boil water to cook it for fear we would be discovered. Sometimes we caught and ate grasshoppers. But most of the time we had nothing at all. And even if a man managed to come out of a battle alive, more than likely he would be missing a leg or an arm. There was no medicine for us. Only a few little herbs, and morphine for the officers. But we said *nothing!* We did not complain. We fought until we dropped like flies. For our country, for Vietnam."

"I suffered the same thing. The North was not that much better off."

"The same, you say? You had uniforms and tanks and fancy Russian rifles. We wore farmer's rags and used glass and rocks for bullets, if we were so lucky even to have guns. But *that* is not what I am complaining about. We said nothing about using our bare hands. We said nothing when we saw villagers torch their crops and their huts to keep us from having food. My own cousin's village treated me like an enemy, although I was fighting for *their* freedom."

75

Loi's heart began to pound harder as the argument intensified. Dinh scooted closer, and she could feel his body trembling.

"Has Father gone insane?" he whispered. "Has he forgotten who he is talking to? We have to stop him before he says anything worse."

"I think it's too late, Dinh. I've heard these words before. Nothing will stop him now. And I for one hope he spews out all the hatred for the government he has been storing in his heart all these years. Maybe then Hiep will not want to marry me. Go ahead, Uncle Long, tell him all your pain. Tell him," Loi whispered and clasped her hands together as she watched her uncle tottering above Hiep.

"We fought and bled and died because we believed in Uncle Ho," Long continued. "We believed we were doing it to free our country from foreign invaders. And when it was over, we would go back to our homes, live quiet lives, marry lovely girls, and raise healthy children. I wanted to be a scholar, not a soldier. Don't you understand?"

"I understand you are too ungrateful." Hiep staggered to his feet to grab Long's shoulder but missed his mark and fell back down.

"No! I am not finished. When the war was finally over and we threw our useless guns aside and returned to our villages . . . nothing was there. Nothing remained. Instead of helping us rebuild a future, the Party sent us to strange places; tore families apart; told us we did not own the land, we did not own the water buffaloes, we did not even own the chickens and fish anymore. It all belonged to the Party. Before the war, my family had a good home. Now, look at this . . ." He kicked an empty bowl and sent it flying across the hut. "Is this what I fought for? Is this what my father died for—hungry children and women who give birth to two-headed babies? My father's body was never found. No one knows where or when he died. We cannot even honor his death day or prepare his gravesite for festivals. When he left, he said he was going to fight the French, for the freedom of our country. Like him, I would have done anything, made any sacrifice for freedom. But where is our freedom now?" Uncle Long grabbed Hiep's shirt and lifted him to his feet.

"Watch your tongue! No one has an easy life. Everyone has suffered and sacrificed for freedom. I have medals . . ." Hiep reached into his pocket and drew out a handful of medals on faded ribbons. Uncle Long released him and rushed across the room to the altar. He seized a fistful of similar medals and shook them in front of Hiep's face, then threw them on the floor.

"I fought for freedom, not for medals. I fought so that all my countrymen could be free, not just a few fat pigs in the Party."

"Say no more! We are soon to be related by marriage, but I cannot tolerate treason."

"Marriage! Ha! I would rather see my niece married to that penniless buffalo boy than to a hypocritical Party member who steals from the slaving farmers."

Loi's back stiffened, and she heard her cousin gasp. They clung to each other's hands and trembled.

"Enough! Now you have gone too far, my friend! I have been a patient man, but this is much too serious. You have already consented to the marriage. Loi and her mother have already accepted the engagement jewelry. It would be dishonorable to back out now."

"What do you know of honor?" Loi's uncle swung his fist toward Hiep and hit the officer's face with a loud smack. Loi screamed and jumped up just as Hiep seized Long's arm and twisted it easily behind him.

"I swear, if you do not consent to the marriage, I *will* report you to the village council. You have been of questionable loyalty for a long time, but I overlooked it because of your niece. But if you withhold her from me, there is no reason for me to look the other way any longer. Do you want to be shipped to the camp at Long Binh for reeducation? Your sister and children would become paupers—outcasts and beggars in the street."

"Better that than being cowards of the Party."

"So, you still refuse to allow the marriage?"

"I will always refuse. . . ."

"No!" Loi screamed and ran across the room. She dropped to the floor and wrapped her arms around her uncle's waist. "Uncle, please, no! I will marry Officer Hiep. Don't say anything more. I will marry him." A sob wracked her body and she felt the strength of her uncle slowly slipping away.

Officer Hiep smiled slightly, then loosened his grip.

"Well, maybe someone in this family has sense after all." He stood back, straightened his uniform, and reached for his cap.

"You came very close to losing everything tonight. I know it was the wine talking. But all the same, if Loi is not ready for the wedding in one month, you can consider yourself a prisoner of the state."

Hiep crammed the cap down low over his eyes, gave a small bow to Loi, and stomped out of the hut. A moment later his motorcycle roared.

Loi felt her uncle's body trembling with anger, then a cry of rage swelled from his lips as his knee rose under her chin with a force that knocked her to the floor. In three angry strides, he was out the door.

Loi sat up slowly, aware of the pairs of eyes staring at her from the dark corners of the hut. After a moment, a shadowy figure blew out the lantern and helped her to her feet.

"Go to bed, Loi," her mother whispered. "It has been a very, very long day." Loi felt her mother's firm hand on her elbow and the presence of her head at shoulder height. In the darkness Má helped her daughter unfasten her blouse and white pants, and slip back into her faded black *quan*.

Loi laid on the thin straw mattress, expecting her mother to drape the mosquito net over her, but instead the woman leaned over and placed a kiss on Loi's cheek. A sudden recollection of the dream, of the American soldier putting his lips on her mother's cheek, flashed through Loi's mind. Then her mother took Loi's hand in her own and sat on the edge of the cot.

"My daughter, I know you are unhappy with the marriage arrangement. And what you did tonight for Uncle Long was courageous and the proper thing to do. Thank you for saving him from prison. Sometimes you are so troublesome that I wish I had never given birth to you." She paused and drew in a deep breath, then squeezed Loi's hand harder. "You know, the other women in Da Nang told me to twist the umbilical cord around your neck when you were born and throw you into the river. But I kept that cord, like any mother, and buried it in the earth."

"Like my little cousins' cords are buried in our yard now?"

The woman nodded. "But sometimes you are like an angel. It is as if you were sent to me as a test, like the story of the old woman who gave birth to a frog, who much later turned out to be the son of the Jade Emperor."

"Do you think I look like a frog?"

"No, no, no . . . but raising you has not been easy. Someday I would not be surprised to find that you are really the daughter of the Jade Emperor in disguise."

"If I am, Má, then I must have been a very bad daughter in heaven to be punished with such a life as this." Loi's lips trembled as she pulled her hand free from her mother's and rolled onto her side.

The woman rose and unfurled the net over the cot before slipping away on silent feet. Loi stared at the opening in the bamboo wall. Soon a cool breeze pushed the hair off her tear-stained cheeks and carried the fragrance of flowers from the school yard.

Loi had not been able to make herself tell her mother that she had no intention of marrying Officer Hiep. Her trickery had not fooled him, but there was one final resort. And the chance for it would come very soon.

6

THE PLAN

LOI STOOD in the middle of the melon patch, watching the sky. Against the sharp blueness, brightly colored shapes rose and dipped, spun and collided. Even though the kites were flying at the other end of the village, she could hear the laughter of the children and the occasional outburst of cheers from the crowd watching the fights.

If she squinted and cupped her hand over her eyes, Loi could distinguish her cousin Dinh's bright yellow kite. He had painstakingly painted red eyes and black fangs on it, to make it look like a fierce tiger. And for a tail, the gold-and-red silk scarf that Officer Hiep had given her at the engagement party one week ago twitched with the wind.

Loi saw the tiger kite swooping toward a blue-and-green dragon kite, aiming its glass claws for the string. A brief crunch, then cheers as the dragon kite broke free and rose with the wind current until it dropped and crashed into the top of a jujube tree in the school orchard.

Loi smiled. Dinh had been champion last year, and now it looked like he would win the contest again. She would have liked to be there to congratulate him, but today she did not feel lucky and had decided that her cousin's fortune would go better if she remained home and worked in her mother's garden.

Loi glanced around at the rows of melons still to be pulled. Already the ground was piled with the dark green orbs. Even her mother had not expected such a large crop. Loi continued twisting the melons off the vines, occasionally glancing over the top of the bamboo thicket that creaked and moaned and rattled in the breeze. Finally the last kite had been vanquished and only the great yellow tiger arrogantly stalked the sky.

"Loi! Oh, Loi!" A small girl's voice sang out as she came running across the garden. "Dinh won the kite battles again."

Loi received her youngest cousin, Hoa, into her outstretched arms and squeezed the little girl tightly.

"That's wonderful. But now Dinh's head will be so swollen with pride that he'll be impossible to live with for a few days."

The little girl giggled. "But Dinh says he could never have won if you hadn't let him use your new red-and-gold scarf. If Auntie sees your scarf now, she's going to be mad. Didn't you like it?"

"No, I didn't like it, or the man who gave it to me."

"But Auntie says you should be proud of it because it's so expensive. I can't wait for your wedding, Loi. Is it soon?"

"Three very short weeks. Most couples marry in December, but Hiep insisted on a wedding this month, in September. He didn't even consult the astrologers. I know it's an unlucky date."

Loi heard a shout and saw her youngest boy cousin, Tuan, tearing down the garden path. "Dinh won the kite fight!" He huffed. "But your scarf is all dirty. Are you going to beat him up?" His bright eyes twinkled as he grabbed a ripe tomato and sank his teeth into it, which was no easy task since his front two teeth were missing.

"Oh, maybe I'll overlook his carelessness this time, since he won. I wasn't very fond of that scarf anyway. I told Má she could keep it."

"When are we going to market with the vegetables?"

"As soon as we get all these washed off and loaded up into the wagon. Probably tomorrow."

"I can't wait!" Tuan jumped into the air, then did a few somersaults and pretended to be fighting an imaginary enemy with kung fu. His skinny arms and legs stuck out like bamboo sticks as he punched and kicked the air and did flips on the ground. Then he grabbed a piece of bamboo and attacked his younger sister, who screamed and ran behind Loi for protection. Loi knocked the stick from his hand, then picked it up and pointed it at his chest.

"Now I've got you, evil one."

"Oh, no, you don't. I've just changed into a snake. Hsss."

He slithered in the grass, his small body twisting from side to side. Loi broke into laughter, but her heart felt heavy. She was going to miss her little cousins. The thought of never seeing them again, of not watching them grow up or helping them through the hurts and bruises and disasters and kite fights, saddened her. If only she could marry Khai, she could live in the same village and be with them all forever.

"Loi, is it time to start making the *long-den* for the Moon Festival yet?" Tuan suddenly asked.

"Yes, we can start the lanterns today. But first I will need some dry bamboo. Very small pieces. And we'll have to find some pretty colored rice paper left over from last year's lanterns. Or maybe from one of those ruined kites."

"Tell me again when the festival is?"

"In about twelve days. On the night of the first full moon of this month. Má will know the exact day. Don't worry, she won't forget."

"Are you going to help make the moon cakes this

year?" Hoa asked as she straddled the biggest melon in the patch.

Loi looked into the small, sweet face and felt pain wrench her heart. How could she tell the children that she would not be here to make the moon cakes, to watch the lantern parade, to tell them fairy tales out under the yellow moon on the night of the festival? She didn't want to lie, yet she could tell no one her plan. No one except Khai. For Khai was part of her plan. She smiled and scooped the girl up into her arms.

"We'll see. Maybe Má will ask *you* to help her make the moon cakes this year, or to fry the watermelon seeds."

The small children soon grew tired of helping Loi and skipped away to help cut flowers from the school yard to sell at market. Loi gathered the rest of the vegetables, then washed, dried, and separated baskets of melons, cucumbers, tomatoes, cabbages, radishes, mangoes from the forest, and bunches of betel leaves.

As the sun sank low and the long slanted shadows turned to darkness, Loi took the *don ganh* from the wall, fitted it with water baskets, and trotted to the well. The tangy smells of lemon grass and damp earth filled her nostrils as she stepped off the path and ran to the place she and Khai had agreed to meet. He was already waiting, his tall body leaning against a flame tree. Even in the dusk, the tree's brilliant red flowers showed color.

"Tomorrow is the day," she whispered. "My mother said the villagers will take their goods to Da Lat early in the morning. Have you convinced your father to let you go?"

"Yes. He finally said I could go along and try to sell my wood carvings. But he thinks it is useless and swears that if I come back empty-handed, he will throw all the figurines into the fire."

"What about your older brother, Quy?"

"I think he's envious of me getting to take a day off. They're starting to burn off the stubble in the rice fields tomorrow and the smoke always makes Quy sick. But Father wants him to stay."

"Then it is set. We will go to Da Lat and help sell vegetables. And while the families load up to return, we will fake my accidental death, then run away and get married."

"It's the only thing left to do, Loi. I cannot stand by and watch you marry that swine Hiep. And I heard my brother and mother talking about finding a wife for me. They both agreed that Suong was a logical choice."

"Suong? With the missing tooth and thick eyebrows? Surely not. She . . . she acts so strange. She admits to wandering about at night and talking to spirits. I'm afraid of her evil eyes."

"I know, and I agree. But her father is a member of the village council, don't forget."

Loi sighed, then touched Khai's hand. It felt warm and strong.

"Perhaps Suong should marry Officer Hiep."

Khai grinned, his white teeth glistening in the pale light of the crescent moon. "They would be a perfect match," he said with a chuckle.

Loi tried to join in his laughter, but all she could think of was the trip tomorrow and her future.

"Khai . . . are we doing the right thing?" she asked in a trembling voice. "I've wrestled with this plan every night. It's all I think of. In many ways it's far worse than a real death—not being able to see my family again. Is it too . . . too dishonorable to go against my uncle's wishes?" She looked up into Khai's dark eyes, praying for his consent to her plan.

He sighed, then sat beneath the flame tree. "Yes, it is dishonorable to disobey your Uncle Long. But . . . it would be far worse if you just ran away and left him to face prison. If you fake your death, then Officer Hiep cannot hold it against your family. And *that* is an honorable result."

A rush of affection flowed over Loi as she looked into Khai's kind face. Her heart raced as she struggled to form the words to tell him how much she loved him and his compassionate ways.

"Khai, it is your future, too, that we are ruining. If you have any second thoughts—"

He held up his finger to quiet her lips. "You are the one taking the most risk, Loi. For the youngest son to leave home is expected, but for a daughter to run away from a marriage is almost unforgivable. But only time will tell." He took her hand and squeezed it. Loi felt the heat of a blush sweeping over her face.

"It's getting late. I must hurry and fetch water. Maybe we can ride together in the wagon tomorrow. If not, I will talk to you when we arrive at the marketplace."

"Till tomorrow, Loi," Khai whispered.

"Till tomorrow," she replied, then slid her hand from his.

Early the next morning Loi helped her mother press out wet patties of sticky rice between banana leaves for the long trip. While her mother's back was turned, Loi slipped a few patties into a small cloth sack, along with a few radishes and a tomato. The night before, she had removed the photograph from under the family altar and taken the teakwood water buffalo from beside her bed. She had no other possessions.

Long before the eastern horizon turned pale gray, the villagers hitched their oxen to wooden carts and began loading the carts by lantern light. All the while Loi hoisted baskets of vegetables, her eyes scanned the path down which Khai would be coming. Soon the water buffaloes passed by, the younger buffalo boys angry because they were not allowed to go to market. But Khai was not among them.

In the palest of gray light, the carts began to rumble down the rocky path and women settled down beside their precious cargoes, but still Khai had not shown up, and Loi's heart began to sink. How could she go through with her plan without Khai? Without him, life would not be worth living.

"Loi, hurry up and climb into the cart," her mother demanded. "Are you going to walk all the way to market?"

"I just want to walk a few minutes longer, Má. Sitting in the wagon makes my legs cramp."

"Hmmmph," her mother snorted, then she began chattering with the other women, comparing the sizes of their vegetables.

The carts rolled slowly up a hill, so Loi had no trouble keeping up. Soon the sky turned into a water-color of pinks, purples, and streaks of gold. Each time she turned around, the brightness of the east hit her eyes, but she could still see the dark outline of the village and the empty road leading from it.

As the carts reached the top of the hill and began to descend, Loi had to trot to keep up. Sweat began to bead up on her face and stream down her back, and her breath grew shorter. She would not be able to stand the pace much longer.

"Loi, come into the cart," her mother said angrily. "Come up here now."

Reluctantly, Loi took her mother's outstretched hand and leapt up between her two youngest cousins. Her long legs dangled over the back of the cart and her feet almost dragged on the ground.

"I know why you were walking," her cousin Tuan said, his eyes twinkling with the importance of his secret.

"Oh? Why?"

"That's why." Tuan pointed a finger at a tiny figure running down the road toward them.

"Khai!" Loi whispered, then let out a long breath.

The children cheered the figure running down the road, and Loi clapped her hands. But as the cart stopped, she saw another figure running toward them, too. As Khai paused beside the cart, his eyes met hers and she saw a little flame of anger. His brother Quy staggered up, leaned on the wagon to catch his breath, then put his hand on Khai's shoulder and pushed him toward the other cart.

"There's no room for you on that cart, little brother," Quy said as his black eyes flashed into Loi's. She had seen that same look many times before in the eyes of a hawk guarding its nest. It was a look that could only mean trouble.

7

THE ESCAPE

THE OX carts bumped along the dirt road until they reached Route 11. If they turned south, they could go to the coastal town of Phan-rang. Loi had been there three times already, and the thought of getting to swim in the South China Sea and play on the white beaches, while the waves rose and fell, made her smile. She still had some seashells that she had found washed ashore. But best of all, vendors sold *nuoc chanh*, cool lime-and-sugar drinks, beneath the coconut palms. But if they turned north, they would come to beautiful Da Lat, the City of Love, where honeymooners strolled under whispering pines.

As the carts approached the highway and stopped, the adults began to argue about which direction to go. Some preferred to go to Phan-rang, which was an easier journey with its flatter terrain. But others insisted on going to Da Lat, where foreign tourists and vacationing Vietnamese often stayed. Their goods would fetch more money there, but that road was up the mountains, a grueling climb over Ngoan Muc Pass.

Finally the arguing stopped and the carts slowly turned toward Da Lat. Loi settled back against the edge of the cart and watched the scenery moving by. Even though the sun had risen, the mists still swirled in the valleys and low places on the road, giving the landscape a haunted, eerie feeling. The higher they climbed, the heavier the mists became, until it felt as if they were riding through the clouds. One time they passed a group of Montagnard tribespeople on foot carrying fishing nets and frames. The women wore long wraparound skirts and had babies strapped to their backs. They stared in silence as the carts rumbled past. Another time a faded and rusty green bus chugged by, its horn beeping. The top rack contained every kind of item imaginable—bicycles, baskets, trunks, even people who couldn't find seats inside. Several women held ducks or chickens upside down by their legs and dangled them out the bus windows.

When the ox carts arrived at the bottom of a steep mountain, everyone climbed out and walked. Khai and the other boys pushed the carts from behind. Loi tried to walk beside him, but Quy gave her an angry glance and biting insult. At the top of Ngoan Muc

Pass, the boys crumpled to the ground, damp with sweat, and the women took out some cold rice and tea.

Loi saw Khai standing on the edge of the mountain, looking over the distant misty valleys and hills below. She stepped up beside him and gave him one of the rice patties from her cloth bag and a cup of tea.

"I'm sorry Quy came," he whispered as he stared straight ahead. "He convinced Father that I couldn't be trusted with money, that I would get cheated by shrewd tourists."

"Does he suspect anything between us?"

"No. I'm sure he just wanted to get out of burning off the stubble in the fields." Khai smiled as he handed Loi the empty cup. "Don't worry."

Loi's heart took courage from his smile. She knew that once the villagers had set up their stalls and baskets of goods, Quy would be too busy to watch Khai every moment of the day.

Half an hour later, the carts were rolling again. The air grew cooler, and the smell of crisp pine trees drifted on the breeze. Now and then they saw farmers spreading their rice on the highway for drying. A few women tossed sugarcane stalks under the wheels of the passing carts to break the tough stems. The sweet odor stuck to the wheels and made Loi think once again of the lime-and-sugar drinks served along the beach.

Just outside of Da Lat, Loi noticed large houses

made of white stucco with wooden trim and brick chimneys peeping out from the tops of orange-red tile roofs.

"Auntie, why are those houses so funny looking?" Loi's cousin Hoa asked. "Who lives there?"

"Those are called villas. They were built by rich Frenchmen long before you or I were born. During the hot summers, the owners would come here from Saigon to get away from the heat. If you look very hard, way over there, you can see the summer palace of Emperor Bao Dai. He came here every year to hunt wild game and tigers."

"Tigers?" Tuan squirmed and stood up, his eyes squinting to mere slits. "I don't see any tigers."

"That's because they live in the mountain jungles. But often tigers would come to the farm villages and eat the cattle and pigs. Whenever that happened, the farmers would petition the emperor for help. And Emperor Bao Dai himself would get his hunting rifles and servants and go into the jungles like it was a big party. He would bring along his friends, several girlfriends, and lots of fine food and wine. He was an expert marksman and one year killed over thirty tigers."

"Where are the tigers now?" Tuan asked.

"Most of them died in the last war," Loi's mother replied, and the little boy heaved a long sigh.

Soon the outline of Da Lat peeked between the pine-covered hills. Rows of houses, some covered in

95

white stucco, others bare and ugly, rose in steps along the hillsides. Farmers on foot, loaded down with fruit, vegetables, and livestock, crowded the narrow road. An old woman guided a small flock of ducks that squawked and honked and caused a traffic jam. Small piglets squealed and grunted protest at being caged inside bamboo baskets hanging from *don ganhs*. One man was carrying what looked like his entire vegetable garden on top of his bicycle. He walked beside it, steering the handle with one hand and holding it upright with a metal pole attached to the seat.

The noise and hubbub rose to a crescendo as the villagers chatted merrily. Loi and her cousins climbed down and ran to the shores of the beautiful blue lake that occupied the center of town. The wind swooshing through the pine trees gave it its name, Whispering Lake. Loi dipped her hands into the cool water and splashed it over her face, while the adults argued over where to set up stalls.

Loi prayed that Khai would sit near her family, but Quy convinced his young brother to station himself in front of the grand white stucco Dalat Palace Hotel. This was where most tourists and honeymooners stayed, and Quy was sure they would want to buy Khai's teakwood carvings as souvenirs.

The rest of the villagers carried their goods to the central marketplace, a huge two-story complex. Loi breathed in the sweet fragrance of fresh fruit and hundreds of cut flowers from the lower-level stalls, where her mother settled down. Other villagers, who had hard goods, and mountain tribespeople with handmade crafts and with babies on their backs went to the upper floor.

At first, Loi was so busy helping her mother she didn't have time to think about her escape plan. But by noon, her mother was in a happy mood and agreed to let her look around the town while everyone was napping.

"Auntie, can we go out in one of those paddle-boats on the lake?" asked Hoa. "Or ride a pony? Please."

"No, I want to go look at the big waterfalls," said Tuan. "Maybe we'll see a wild tiger there."

Loi's mother shook her head. "Tst, tst. Those waterfalls are too dangerous for little children. The rocks are as slippery as an eel's back. But maybe you can have a ride in one of the boats or on a pony, if it doesn't cost too much. And if Loi will watch over you." Loi's mother took several fifty-*dong* bills from her pocket and handed the money to Loi. "Be shrewd with the money, Loi," she called out as Loi took each child's hand and felt herself being dragged toward the lake.

As they passed the Dalat Palace Hotel, Loi saw Khai sitting alone on the wide, terraced steps.

"Where is Quy?" she asked as the children broke away.

"He's eating at that restaurant," Khai replied, pointing toward a romantic pavilion that jutted out over the blue waters.

"He's wasting his money, but I'm glad he's gone. I've been thinking about our plan." She glanced at the children to make sure they were out of earshot. They had cornered a teenage boy riding a small horse and were busy stroking its shaggy coat.

"So have I," Khai replied. "I have a good idea how to fake your death and leave no trace of a body."

"Good. Let me hear it." But before Khai could explain, some fair-skinned tourists in strange clothes walked toward them.

"Are those the kind of people who have been buying your carvings?" Loi asked, unable to keep from staring.

"No. The others were Vietnamese. Mostly honeymooners."

The strangers towered over their Vietnamese guide and translator. One tourist held a camera in front of his face and carried several black leather bags slung over his shoulder. He pointed his camera at everything, no matter how ordinary. The sound of little whirs filled the air around him like the buzzing of a hive of bees. His skin was light and his eyes were blue, but Loi could not take her gaze off the brown hair growing all over his face.

"Is he part bear?" she whispered to Khai, and they

both giggled under their breath. Loi's heart began to pound louder as the two men stopped in front of Khai's display. She didn't want to be rude and tried not to stare, but she had never seen such funny clothing. Both men wore pants that had been cut off at the knees, revealing sunburned legs covered with pale, curly hairs. And their feet were as big as boats. The man with the camera wore a brightly colored flowered shirt, and the other wore a pale blue shirt and matching floppy cloth hat the same color as his eyes.

Loi tried to keep her eyes downcast, but the Vietnamese guide spoke directly to her.

"Miss, what is your name?" he asked.

"Pham Thi Loi."

The taller man spoke to the guide. His voice was soft, and though Loi didn't understand what he was saying, she suddenly had a flash of her dream. The words had the same kind of sound as the words spoken by the American soldier in her dream. She glanced up quickly to look into his face. The stranger was looking directly at her, his blue eyes unblinking. He was so tall she could hardly see the top of his head, but she could see curly reddish hair peeking from under his floppy blue bush hat.

"Excuse me, Miss Loi, this man wants to know if your father was an American soldier?"

Loi swallowed hard, and her heart thumped against her rib cage. She glanced at Khai for advice, but his own eyes were wide with wonder.

"Please, Miss Loi, answer the question." The interpreter's tone was far less patient sounding than the stranger's.

"Yes . . . my father was an American soldier."

"This man wants to know how old you are and what your mother's name was."

Loi rose to her feet and stepped back, almost stumbling over a basket.

"Why? Why does this stranger want to know about me? I've never seen him before."

The guide made unpleasant clicks with his tongue and shook his head.

"Behave yourself, please. You have nothing to fear. This man is an American. He was a soldier here in 1969 and is looking for his own child and the woman he lived with. The child would have been born around Cam Ranh Bay."

Loi expelled her breath slowly and pushed back a curl that had fallen across her face. She noticed that her fingers trembled.

"Tell the American that I am not his daughter. I was born in 1972—the Year of the Rat. I am the daughter of Pham Thi Lan, and I was born in Da Nang." She thrust her chin up and looked the stranger in the eyes, while the guide made a quick translation. She saw the blue eyes above her slowly lose their twinkle and grow sad. The man's mouth turned down at the corners and a long, heavy sigh slipped from his lips. Then he reached into his pocket and removed a photograph. It was much larger and in better condition than the one Loi carried inside the cloth pouch slung around her neck.

"The American wants to know if you have ever seen this woman."

Loi stared at the picture of a pretty woman standing beside the tall American. He was very young then, but he had the same curly red hair and his teeth were big and white in a tanned face. Loi felt a sudden sadness in her heart and passed the photo over to Khai.

"Have you ever seen this woman?"

Khai shook his head. Loi handed the photo back to the American.

"Tell him I am very sorry. I wish he were my father, but I know he isn't. I have a photograph, too." Loi fished out the faded piece of blue silk and carefully unwrapped it from the photo. She held the picture up to the American. He removed a pair of plastic-framed glasses from his shirt pocket, then took the photo in his hand and studied it carefully. All the time she looked into his face she relived her dream over and over, remembering the smiling blue eyes that had filled with tears.

The stranger spoke for several minutes in his odd, flat language. Loi turned toward the guide in anticipation. "The American says to tell you his name is Raymond Smith," the guide said. "He works for a large American magazine and is writing a story about children of American soldiers. He is also looking for his own daughter, Mai, who would be about nineteen or twenty by now. His friend wants to take your photograph for the magazine. They say you are very beautiful."

Loi blushed and looked at Khai. He nodded.

The hairy man with the camera buzzed around her a few minutes, snapping shot after shot, asking her to stand, to sit, to hold something, to push her hair back, to smile, to frown. Then he handed her a package of American cigarettes and said, "Thank you."

Loi stared at the package of Marlboros. They were worth as much as a day's salary. She didn't know if he wanted her to take just one or the whole package. She didn't smoke, but cigarettes were as good as money. She could trade them for food.

"*Thank you*," she said in English, imitating the cameraman.

Raymond Smith began speaking to Loi again. This time he squatted down to her level and placed his hand on her shoulder.

"Mr. Smith is asking you if you have heard about the Amerasian Homecoming Program between the American and Vietnamese governments," the guide explained.

"No," Loi replied.

"He says any child of an American soldier can come to the United States. The American government will pay for everything and find you sponsors and a place to live. All you have to do is prove your father was American. In your case it wouldn't be too hard, because of the curly hair and freckles. If you're married, your husband and children can come, too. And of course, your mother. He says you might even be able to locate your father, because he can see the division number on the soldier's left sleeve in the photo—the same division he was in."

Loi's heart drummed so loudly in her ears that she could hardly hear the guide's words.

"He says you need to go to Ho Chi Minh City to register at the Foreign Office."

"Ho Chi Minh City . . . you mean Saigon?" Loi asked.

"Yes, it was called Saigon under the old regime. But you would be wise to call it by its correct name, in honor of Uncle Ho," the guide said firmly.

The two Americans spoke to each other a few minutes, then the tall one picked up a teak carving. He reached into his wallet and removed a fistful of money. "How much?"

Before Khai could answer, Loi pushed the figurine into the man's large hands. "For you, it is free."

The man argued and argued, until they finally agreed that he would not pay for the figurine, but he gave her a pack of 555 brand cigarettes.

"Good luck, Loi," Raymond Smith said with a big grin as he waved good-bye.

"Good luck to you, too, Raymond Smith," she called out. As the men walked away, Loi turned and seized Khai's forearms.

"Khai, do you know what this means? With these cigarettes and the money you've earned from selling the figurines, we will have enough money to buy tickets to Saigon."

"Saigon. But . . . that's so far away. And so big. I thought we would settle down not far from Da Lat. We could farm, and I could sell carvings from time to time. Why do we need to go all the way to a big city like Saigon?"

"You heard what the American Raymond Smith said. I can go to America for free. And if we're married, you can come with me. And even Má can come with us. We can start a fresh life, away from all the humiliation and pain I face every day. My curly hair and freckled nose wouldn't be so strange there. And he said we might find my father. I can't believe it."

"But what about me, Loi? All I know how to do is tend water buffaloes and farm rice. Do you think there are rice farms in America?"

Loi sighed. Why was Khai being so stubborn? She forced a smile and seized his hand.

"Of course there are rice farms in America. Everyone has to have rice. But if I find my father, we won't have to worry about that. I'm sure he will help us. Don't you see, I have to find him. I have to know the truth." Loi tried to take Khai's other hand, but he stepped back and crossed his arms. His eyes became dark and moody.

"Maybe I don't want to go to America. My home is here in the provinces; I'm a farmer, not a city dweller."

"But you promised me we would run away and get married," Loi said loudly, then glanced around to make sure her little cousins had not heard. They were still petting the pony. She turned back to Khai, who was staring out toward the lake, his chin set at a stubborn angle.

"I didn't promise I would go to another country or to a big city like Saigon, where people live like ants in a hill. You're being too selfish, Loi. And maybe your mother doesn't want to go, either."

Loi hung her head a moment, twisting the pack of cigarettes in her hands.

"I know we hadn't planned on going to America. But I just thought that as long as we were together, it didn't matter where we lived," she said softly. "I thought maybe my father—"

Khai's heavy sigh interrupted her words.

"I'll have to think about it for a while, Loi," he said. "Give me an hour to make up my mind. And what about the accident we were going to fake for you? I know the perfect way."

"Maybe I won't have to go through with it. Where can I meet you?"

"On the bridge over the dam. In one hour. I will

tell Quy that I'm going to look at the waterfalls on the edge of town."

Loi nodded, then hurried to her cousins. She paid the teenage boy to let the children ride the pony around the lake, then escorted them back to the market, where her mother was just waking from her nap. The vegetables had sold very well, and Má was in a good mood, which made Loi's heart fill with hope.

After the children were asleep, Loi fidgeted with the baskets, rearranged the melons, and paced as she tried to find the courage to speak to her mother.

"Daughter, what is wrong with you?" her mother finally asked.

Loi took a deep breath and dropped to her knees in front of the short woman. She took the tiny hands into her own and squeezed.

"Má," she said in a too-high voice, unable to hide the excitement she felt. "What would you say if I told you that we—you and I—could go to America today? That it would cost us nothing. Would you go?"

A dark cloud passed over her mother's face. For a long time she stared at Loi with eyes that did not see. Then she pulled her hands free.

"Why, child, what would I do in America? I have no family or friends there. I don't speak their strange language. Besides, your Uncle Long needs me. I must take care of his children until he finds another wife.

It's because of me and you that he leads such a sad life. I could never desert him." She cocked her head sideways and studied Loi's face. "Why do you ask such questions, daughter?"

"Má, I saw an American today."

"And how do you know what an American looks like?" Má quickly began shifting the mangoes from one basket to another, then back again, as if her life depended on their arrangement in the shallow container.

"There were two Americans. They are staying at the Palace Hotel and bought a teak carving from Khai."

"Hmmmph! If Americans are here again, that means more trouble is coming, probably."

"But, Má, they told me that you and I could go to America. All we have to do is register in Saigon. Maybe we could find my father—"

Loi's mother interrupted with a wave of her hand. "Hush, hush. Don't ever talk about that man. He doesn't want us. I've told you that before. We mean no more to him than an ant to the elephant."

Loi felt the blood drain from her face and an empty pain in her chest. She slumped to the step and stared at her large hands. After a moment, she saw her mother's shadow. She looked up and saw Má holding a handful of money, smiling.

"My vegetables sold very well today. Take some

money and buy yourself a *nuoc mia*. I saw a vendor squeezing sugarcane over near the lake. You mustn't dwell on things you cannot change, Loi."

Loi saw her mother's delicate hand holding out three bills. As she reached up to take them, Loi noticed that her own fingers trembled. She swallowed several times before she could speak.

"Má, Khai asked me if I could go with him to look at the waterfalls on the edge of town. It won't take long. We'll ride in a pony cart out there."

"Just like honeymooners," her mother said with a sigh and a smile. "All right. I guess it is the last time you and Khai will have a chance to say a proper farewell before your wedding." Her eyes examined Loi's face with a tenderness Loi rarely saw.

"Yes, I think it is important to say good-bye and clear the air for a final time before people part forever," Loi replied softly, trying to hold back her own tears. She wished her mother wasn't being so kind now. Every gentle word, every laugh, only made Loi's heart ache more.

"Now, now, don't be so sad, daughter. You'll see. Marriage won't be as bad as you think. Once you have children of your own, the husband won't matter." She patted Loi's hand. Suddenly Loi threw her arms around her mother's neck and sobbed.

"I love you, Má," she said. Then she leaned over and kissed her two sleeping cousins and ran toward the bridge over the dam.

Khai was already waiting for Loi.

"What did your mother say?" he asked.

Loi shook her head, unable to speak.

"Then do you want to go ahead with the plan to fake your death?"

Loi nodded. "What do I need to do?"

"I'll need something that belongs to you."

"What about my *non-la?*" She started to remove her pointed hat.

"We need something else, too. Everyone has a *non-la.*"

"Ah . . . you can have this red-and-yellow scarf that Officer Hiep gave me. Má insisted I wear this ugly thing around my neck today. But I hate it."

"Good," Khai said as he took her hand and led her toward a waiting pony cart. "I've already paid the driver. Make a big scene so he won't forget seeing you. I'll explain the plan later."

Loi nodded and did her best to make sure the driver noticed her. She tied and removed, tied and removed her red-and-yellow scarf several times, and she spoke in a loud voice about loving the scarf so much she would never part with it.

Soon Loi heard the roar of the grand waterfalls and saw a crowd of people leaning over a wooden platform. Only a few couples had dared to walk down toward the boulders where the water tumbled and smashed like angry white fists.

Again Loi made sure everyone saw her red-and-yellow scarf and would remember her. Then she and Khai carefully climbed down the twisting trail to the slippery rocks.

"Quickly, hide in the bushes over there while no one is looking," Khai said. Loi ducked into a tangle of shrubs while Khai picked his way farther upstream to where the pounding fury of the water was deafening. Through a crack in the bushes, Loi saw him toss her hat into the foamy water, then dip her scarf until it turned dark and limp. Then she heard him scream again and again in a very convincing voice. Soon a few people joined him and began searching the water, following the path of the pointed hat.

As planned, Loi doubled back along the riverbank, hiding in the bushes until it was safe to go back onto the road. She flagged down a three-wheeled pedicab and rode back into town.

Avoiding the marketplace, Loi trotted to a jewelry store she had seen earlier. She yanked the engagement ring off her finger and sold it for cash, thankful that Officer Hiep had such good taste. With part of the money and the entire pack of 555 cigarettes, Loi purchased a new hat and a spot on the roof of the old green DeSoto bus with orange bumpers. The driver was busy refilling its water tank, which was roped on top above the driver's seat. It would be a long, rough ride, and her body would be sore, but her uncle had told her many times that freedom was never easy, so Loi didn't mind.

The next half hour seemed like a lifetime as Loi hid in a stand of tall bamboo, pretending to fish on Whispering Lake. But all the while, she kept one eye on the bus and the other on the road leading toward the waterfalls. She imagined that by now Khai had taken the wet scarf to her mother and told her the bad news. Loi's eyes teared up at the thought of her mother crying and running toward the waterfalls. Khai would have to hold her back and convince her that it was pointless to look anymore. No one could survive the thrashing around on the rocks. Loi wondered if her mother would blame Khai. Would the villagers believe the story? If not, then surely her Uncle Long would go to a reeducation camp for disobeying Officer Hiep.

The mountain air was cool, but it was not the crisp air that made Loi shake and shiver like a dog in a spring rainstorm. Suddenly she heard a loud rumble and a hiss like a weary snake's. She saw passengers begin to load their belongings on top of the old bus—baskets, boxes, and a bicycle tied down to the end.

Two old men had already settled down on top of the bus when Loi arrived at the back bumper. She sat down and stared across the lake at the whispering pine trees and cool, misty mountains. Her heart pounded as she began to think about what she had done and what lay ahead of her. Should she go?

Suddenly she heard her name and leapt to her feet.

"Khai!" she exclaimed as she saw him trotting up, out of breath.

"I'm going with you," he said between gasps for air. "Half the villagers think it was my fault you fell in the waterfall. Quy's mad at me, too, for being so stupid. I felt so lonely, even pretending you were dead. How can I stay behind? Maybe you're right about America."

Loi broke into a wide grin and threw her arms around his neck.

"Hurry, you must go buy a bus ticket at that shop over there. Ask for a seat on top. I'll save a place for you."

As Loi started to climb over the tied-down bike, a blast of dark, oily smoke belched from the tail pipe. Then she felt the bus begin to shudder as the motor turned over several times.

"Please hurry, Khai," she whispered. Her eyes anxiously watched Khai run to the shop and emerge a moment later carrying a piece of paper. She smiled and scooted over to make room for him. Then she heard a familiar voice shouting.

"Wait, Khai!"

Loi turned around and saw Quy swaggering down the road toward his younger brother. He stopped in front of Khai.

"What are you doing now?" he demanded. "Haven't you already gotten into enough trouble for one day?" He jerked the ticket out of Khai's hand, briefly read it, then stuffed it into his pocket. "What are you doing?" he asked in disbelief.

"I'm going to Saigon. Everyone in the village hates me," Khai replied. "With Loi dead, I have no reason to stay anymore. I'm going to find my fortune in a bigger city."

Loi lay as flat as she could on the bus top, hoping Quy would not look up at her.

Quy tilted his head and roared with laughter. "That's about the stupidest thing I've ever heard you say, little brother. Now, what could a simpleminded buffalo boy like you do in a city like Saigon? They would eat you alive in two days' time. And don't worry, no one blames you for the death of that *con-lai*." Quy put his arm around Khai's shoulder and turned him away from the bus.

Loi wanted to scream, but she didn't dare reveal herself or the whole plan would be ruined. She bit her lip and whispered a prayer, over and over. Suddenly the bus belched again, and with a creak and a jerk, it began to roll forward.

"Oh, Khai, hurry. Tell the fool to leave you alone," she whispered and clung to the edge of the bus until her knuckles turned white.

"No!" Khai shouted. "You can't stop me, Quy."

The two brothers began to scuffle. As the bus slowly rolled not more than ten feet from them, Loi saw the expression of shock on Quy's face. She knew that this must be the first time Khai had used force against his older brother.

As the bus picked up speed, Loi's heart raced faster and faster. She climbed to her knees and slid down the back of the bus, holding on to the rope that bound the bike. The two fighting brothers grew smaller and smaller.

"Khai!" she moaned as the bus rocked over bumps and holes in the road. Suddenly, she saw Khai hit his brother so hard that Quy hit the ground and rolled into a ditch.

"Khai!" she shouted, this time at the top of her lungs.

"Wait!" Khai returned the shout as he ran toward the departing bus.

The bus groaned as the driver shifted gears and gave it more gas to go up a small incline. White fumes billowed from its tail pipe, consuming Khai like dragon's breath. Khai's legs pumped faster than Loi had thought possible. She saw him kick off his sandals, and his straw hat bobbed on his shoulder.

Loi extended her body as far as it would go and held out her right hand, while still clinging to the bus with the left one. Khai gained slowly, but just when he was two feet away, the bus crested the hill and started down.

The exhaust blasted into Khai's face and he

coughed. Loi could see tears streaming from his red eyes and hear his labored breathing.

"Khai, I love you," she shouted as she saw him losing ground.

"Wait for me in Saigon," he yelled as the bus pulled away. "I'll catch the next bus and join you. Wait for me, Loi. Promise me you'll wait." Khai staggered to a halt in the middle of the road, gasping for air and coughing. He stumbled to his knees but kept his eyes on the bus.

"Promise me, Loi!" he yelled with his last ounce of energy.

"I promise," Loi shouted back. "I promise."

Loi leaned back against the shaking bicycle and watched as Khai became a tiny black speck. A moment more and he had vanished over the horizon.

8

THE CITY

DUSK DESCENDED over the land as the bus
squealed to a halt in the coastal town of Phan-Thiet.
The passengers sighed with relief, for hereafter they
would be traveling on Highway 1, the largest and best
road in the country.

Loi rubbed her eyes as she sat up, then crawled
down over the bikes and bundles. Her feet had gone
to sleep and now tingled with a million needles. As
he had already done three times before, the bus driver
began removing the empty metal drum that was
roped on top of the bus. In a few minutes he would
come back with a new drum of water and attach a
rubber hose leading to the old, rusty radiator that
could no longer function on its own.

A few passengers unloaded their belongings and
vanished into the deserted streets. But the majority

of them remained around the bus, stretching their legs and relieving their bladders beside nearby bushes.

Loi's stomach rumbled, but she decided not to eat the rice inside the cloth pouch slung around her neck. She didn't know how long it would be before she and Khai would leave for America and didn't want to waste food now. She was hoping the driver would allow those on top to come inside the bus, since there were a few empty seats now, but her hopes sank when she saw a whole new family of passengers begin loading their goods inside the bus.

Loi returned to her spot on top of the bus to rest. Sleep had been impossible so far, due to the potholes and washed-out road. For hours she had watched the cool, pine-covered mountains of Da Lat slowly give way to jungle-covered hills and sweeping plains as the terrain became flatter and lower. Already they had passed harvested rice fields, where farmers were burning off the stubble. Now in the darkness, distant fires glimmered and the constant smoke stung her eyes. From here on, the road would pass through smooth farmlands.

The bus began rolling again, making the night air feel cold against Loi's bare arms. The yellow-orange crescent moon hanging in the sky like a slice of melon reminded Loi of her younger cousins. It would be the first year that she had not helped them with their Moon Festival lanterns and paper toys. She tried not to think of how sad the children would be, thinking that she was dead; and soon she dozed off, dreaming of sweet moon cakes and a yellow tiger kite stalking the sky.

Loi sat up with a jolt as the bus rattled over a steel girder bridge that served both cars and trains. Beneath them, specks of light reflected on the dark water of a large, lazy river. Loi rubbed the sleep from her eyes and noticed that the moon was sinking over the top of a cluster of tall buildings. The light was pale, but she could see outlines of hundreds of structures. They loomed like a herd of elephants in a dark jungle.

"It's so big," she whispered. "I didn't know Saigon was so big."

"So, you've never been here before, huh?" said one of the old men on top of the bus as he gathered his battered suitcase and a basket filled with coconuts.

Loi shook her head, unable to take her eyes off the buildings ahead.

"You mustn't call it Saigon in public," he said. "The government renamed it Ho Chi Minh City in 1975, after the war. Be careful what you say here, especially to the police."

Loi had never seen a policeman, but she nodded as if she understood. Then she pointed to a large building several stories high.

"Is that the emperor's palace?" she asked.

The old man laughed, and so did his companion.

"No, child. That is the old Majestic Hotel. It's awfully rundown now, like everything else in this poor old city." He sighed and gazed down the waterfront street, where people were just beginning to stir.

"I remember when we were only a couple of million people," he said. "Now, they say there are four million. Maybe more. This city is a very sad lady. She's had a lot of heartbreak, and her beauty has faded."

"But her soul is still alive," added the other old man as he struggled down from the roof. The words "four million" rang in Loi's ears as she helped the first old man down and then crawled back up and got his basket of coconuts. He offered her one, but she refused, remembering Huong's two-headed baby.

Some of the passengers had friends or family waiting for them. Others waved down three-wheeled *cyclos*. Loi felt she was in their way as they brushed past her in haste. The cool mountain air had long since been replaced with a hot, humid, breathless kind of air that captured and held on to all the unpleasant odors of the night.

As the gray dawn spread, lights glimmered behind shop windows and Loi was shocked to see that the dark forms she had thought were shrubs or uneven lawns were really people. Along the riverbanks and the hotel grounds, waves of people silently rolled up their sleeping mats and gathered their belongings. Men rose from the sidewalks and the park benches.

Khai had been right; the people here did live like ants in a hill.

As she walked aimlessly, men squatting on their heels in doorways and smoking cigarettes stared at her with yellowish eyes.

"Hey, little farm girl, are you lost?" one whispered and reached out for her arm. "Come inside and live with me," he said with an expulsion of smoke. He laughed. But his laughter turned into a fit of raspy coughing, and Loi heard a woman yelling from the room behind him, followed by a baby's yelps.

Loi began to walk faster, pulling her cloth pouch that contained everything she owned close to her chest. The words "four million" swam in her head as the crowds thickened on the sidewalks, and soon she was bumping elbows. Every head seemed to turn toward her, and every pair of eyes seemed to glare at her bare feet and her too-short baggy black pants. The air was growing thinner, she was sure of it. She broke into a trot toward the river, where it didn't look as crowded.

"Taxi, miss?" a voice called out. When Loi looked up, she saw a young man about twenty years old perched on the seat of an empty *cyclo*, flipping through a tattered newspaper.

"Do you know where the Foreign Office is?" she asked.

The young man studied her a long time, then

neatly folded the small paper and tucked it into his back pocket.

"Sure. It's on Bui Thi Xuan Street. It's a long, dangerous walk for a skinny girl like you. I'll take you. Climb in."

"How much would that cost?"

"Five thousand *dong*. Or one American dollar, if you've got it."

"That's too much." She shook her head and began striding in the direction he had pointed. It could be miles away, if it was on the other side of this city of four million. But after she had gone only a few feet, the young man shouted out.

"Okay, okay. You got a cigarette?"

"Yes. How far will one cigarette take me?"

"For you, because you are so pretty and charming, I'll take you halfway—to the circle across from Central Market. I'm going that direction anyway." He steadied the three-wheeled pedicab while she climbed into the cushioned passenger seat. Loi dug out the package of American cigarettes and fished one Marlboro free, making sure the taxi driver didn't see how many she had left. He rolled it in his fingers, smelled it, and read the label before putting it inside his shirt pocket.

"Where did you get American cigarettes?"

"From an American."

"Ha! Americans don't come to Vietnam anymore."

Loi settled into the cracked, patched leather seat in silence. She didn't feel it was his business how she had gotten the cigarettes. Besides, her mother had taught her it was better not to tell everything you knew to a stranger. Always hold something back, in case he turns out to be untrustworthy.

The upholstery of the *cyclo* was ripped, but compared to the roof of the bus, it felt soft and comfortable. Relief flooded over Loi's stiff muscles as she sank back and let the world glide by. She wanted to close her eyes and sleep, but the taxi driver clanged his bell incessantly and didn't even try to avoid the jarring potholes. And, worst of all, he seemed determined to maintain a head-on collision course with every other bicycle, *cyclo*, and motor scooter on the avenue. But, miraculously, each driver or pedaler seemed able to read the mind of the other, and with only a nod of the head to show where each wanted to go, they all kept their vehicles from colliding.

"Where is everyone going in such a hurry?" she asked the driver as a city bus passed by, bulging with men and women dressed in neat pants and shirts.

"To work. To eat. To buy things," he said as he slowed down in front of a *cong-vien*, a small circular park with a statue in the center. It looked like an island of flowers and benches surrounded by a sea of traffic. The driver came to a stop, then pulled out the cigarette and lit it up. "You have a lot to learn about the big city, country girl," he said as he exhaled a long stream of smoke.

Loi felt her cheeks burning as the young man tilted his head back and laughed.

"Why are you here, anyway?" he asked. "Where is your family?"

"I'm going to the Foreign Office to register so I can go to America. That's where my father lives."

"Does your father know you're coming?"

Loi shook her head. "No. I don't even know his name. But I'm sure I can find him. I have his photograph."

The taxi driver held his side and laughed again. Then he stubbed out the cigarette and put the half-smoked butt back into his pocket.

"I'm sorry, country girl," he finally said, and his dark eyes stopped laughing. "But you have so much to learn. It would be better for you if you sold your pack of cigarettes for a bus ticket back to your little village."

Loi swallowed hard and looked at her dirty feet.

"I can't go back," she said softly, then drew in a deep breath. "Am I far from the Foreign Office now?"

"Oh, you are a stubborn one, aren't you?" He grinned a large white smile. "Okay, country girl. Just follow that church steeple to your left. When you get there, ask someone where the Foreign Office is. But be careful."

"Thank you," Loi said, forcing a smile.

"My name is Hung," he said as he began to pedal off into the traffic. "I come to this circle every morning. I'll be waiting to take you back to the bus station," he shouted over his shoulder as he waved and was swallowed up in the mass of bicycles.

Loi took a deep breath and looked around. To her right was a large, pale yellow building with a red tile roof topped by a massive clock tower. She had never seen such a large marketplace and imagined the thousands of goods sold inside. The buildings were much larger than the ones in Da Lat. Down one of the eight streets that radiated from the *cong-vien,* purple bougainvilleas spilled over the balconies of white stucco apartments, and clothes fluttered from wires strung from rooftops.

Loi tried to step across the nearest street, but the swishing bicycles and humming motorbikes kept darting around the corner one after the other without cease. It was a bad time to cross the street, she decided, so she sat on a park bench and took a rice patty from her cloth sack. She was so weak and hungry that her fingers shook as she peeled the banana leaf off and ate the cold sticky rice.

After an hour, Loi concluded that the traffic was not going to slow down. She darted across the street, causing a barrage of bicycle bells and shouts, and walked in the direction of the strange needle-sharp steeple that rose above the trees. Anytime she took a wrong turn, or found herself lost and confused, she would search the sky until she saw the steeple again. Soon it seemed like the beckoning arm of an old friend.

As Loi crossed a long, wide avenue divided by a flower-lined esplanade and rows of tall tamarind trees with whitewashed trunks, she thought how clean and lovely the city looked. In the bright sunlight nothing seemed strange or dangerous. The people were not staring at her after all, as they bustled about and minded their own business. Underneath trees, barbers snipped hair from men reading papers; repairmen tinkered over bikes in the middle of sidewalks; and a crew of women with scarves around their faces patched potholes with buckets of smelly hot tar.

But as Loi continued to walk, the streets grew more narrow and the shops more shabby. Loud, strange music blared from an opened door, and Loi stopped to gawk at the merchandise crammed into the small shop and spilling out onto the sidewalk. She had never seen anything like it before and couldn't imagine what all the shiny pieces of metal were used for. She could see no musicians playing instruments.

"Hey, missy—wanna buy a stereo? Tape deck? How about a color TV? Sony brand. Or maybe you wanna hear some American tapes. I've got plenty, all new—Bruce Springsteen. Madonna. You name it, we've got it." A teenage boy, who was twisting and rocking to the loud music, grinned at her. Suddenly his smile disappeared.

"Hey, you got money or not? No, I guess not. Then get away, *bui-doi!*" Loi stumbled back as he flipped the volume up on the tape player. She bumped into an older lady carrying a wooden tray filled with cigarettes.

"Watch out, *bui-doi!*" she hissed and shoved Loi aside.

Why were they calling her *bui-doi*, dust of life? It sounded as hateful as *con-lai*, Loi thought as she walked faster, squeezing through the crowd, aware that eyes were staring at her. At a corner she leaned against a street lamp to catch her breath. She felt something and looked down to see a gnarled hand on her knee. With a cry of horror, she jumped back.

"Please help me. I need money for my starving family. Buddha will bless you for helping." The old white-haired man whined out the words over and over in a singsong voice, while his film-covered eyes stared ahead in blindness. He had no legs below the knees, and his black pants were tattered where he had dragged his stumps on the ground. A raggedy, skinny girl of about ten was selling paper flowers a few feet away, but no one was buying. When she saw Loi staring at the old man, she ran up and shoved her.

"Keep away from my grandfather, thief," she said in a squeaky, sharp voice.

"I'm not a thief. I-I feel sorry for your grand-father. What happened to him?"

"He lost his legs in the American War. Your father was an American, huh? Maybe your father was the one who blew off old Grandfather's legs. Give him money so he can eat today."

Loi reached into her pouch and fished out a single cigarette.

"This is all I can spare," she said and placed it in the hand of the old man who was now tugging at another pedestrian.

"*Cam on co.*" The old man thanked her and grinned a toothless smile. As he bowed, the skinny girl grabbed the cigarette from his gnarled hand and ran faster than a rabbit into the crowd. The old man frowned and felt around on the sidewalk.

"Where's my cigarette?" he whimpered.

"Your granddaughter took it," Loi explained.

"Granddaughter? I don't have a granddaughter!" He angrily slapped his bony chest. "That girl-thief stole from an old cripple again! Today's children have no respect for their elders." He began to sob bitterly.

Loi sighed as she looked into the crowd that had swallowed up the ragged girl. "And I guess you didn't lose your legs in the American War, either?"

The beggar shook his head. "A bus ran over me ten years ago. The doctor cut my legs off. You have another cigarette, pretty, nice girl? Buddha will bless you." He tugged at her knees.

Loi handed him another cigarette and counted the number left in the pack. As she walked away, Loi pushed her hair up under her hat and crammed it low on her head, vowing not to look up again until she arrived at the Foreign Office. She would register and wait for Khai to join her so they could marry and go to America. The sooner she got out of this city, the better.

9

JOE

A DEEP WEARINESS pressed on Loi's shoulders as she dragged her feet through the crowded streets. During the past twenty-four hours, she had slept no more than three hours, and it had been a restless sleep at that. Now, faced with the uncertainty of her future, she found it more and more difficult to lift her feet.

When Loi finally reached the building with the tall steeple, she felt as if she had come to a roadside rest stop during a long journey. She sank into the cool grass under a tall eucalyptus tree in a small park across the street from the massive stone building with the stained-glass windows. Not far from her feet, clumps of bright yellow chrysanthemums filled the air with their musty fragrance and a cluster of red bottlebrush trees attracted hordes of honeybees.

As the dappled light flickered across her eyes and a light breeze lapped away her perspiration, Loi began to think about Khai. He had said he would catch the next bus to Saigon. She wasn't sure when that would be, but surely no more than one day. Da Lat was a popular tourist town to which many Saigonese traveled for vacations or honeymoons. But once he arrived in Saigon, how would they find each other? Should she wait for him at the bus station, or should she go ahead and register at the Foreign Office and wait for him there? Khai had heard the American tell her that was the place to go; maybe he would try to find her there as soon as he arrived. Loi began to relive the last time she had seen Khai and the look of pain in his eyes as he reached for her fingers. She whimpered under her breath, then fell into the deep sleep of exhaustion.

Loi wasn't sure how long she had been sleeping when something scampered across her chest. Her dream told her it was the rats that often tried to steal her mother's rice bag from a pole in the little hut. Loi smiled in her sleep, thinking she was once again on the cot next to her cousins. But then the scamper became a rough pain on the back of her neck, as if someone were pulling her hair. With a little cry, she sat up and rubbed her stinging neck.

For a moment Loi didn't understand where she was. She heard fleeing footsteps and saw a boy with orange-colored hair running across the park carrying something in his hand. Loi stood but something felt wrong. She glanced down at her chest.

"My sack!" she cried in terror.

With a shot of speed, Loi took off after the boy. He had a good lead on her, but her legs were long and used to running down the country lanes after rabbits and dogs. She leapt over the short wrought-iron fence of the park, cutting in and out of the flower beds. Her heart pounded in her ears and her lungs filled to capacity with hot air. All the while she chased the culprit, she chastised herself for being so stupid as to leave her cloth pouch in plain sight while she slept. She knew better than that. She also knew better than to leave the money and cigarettes in the sack; they should have been safely tucked inside her secret pocket. But worst of all, the photo of her American father wrapped in the piece of blue silk was in that pouch, carelessly shoved back in after the last time she looked at it. She would never, never forgive herself for losing that. Without the photo, how could she prove to the authorities that she was half American?

With a fear greater than she had ever known, even greater than the time she had confronted a cobra in the rice paddy, Loi found a second wind and caught up with the boy as he tripped over a man working on a broken bicycle in the middle of the sidewalk. With a scream, Loi stretched her long arms toward the boy's neck and seized his shirt collar.

"Help! Murder! Murder!" he shouted in a

squeaky voice that was in the throes of changing from boy to man.

A few people laughed, but no one seemed to believe him. The bike repairman cursed and threatened to crack the boy's head open with his wrench.

"Give me back my pouch, or you will be crying more than murder," Loi said between clenched teeth as she tried to get a better hold on his twisting, skinny body.

"You're crazy, girl! This is my bag. My poor old widowed mother sewed it up for me a year ago. I carry it with me all the time."

"Ha! You little liar. Tell me what's inside it."

"Uh—" He held it close to his face. "Rice!" His eyes twinkled as he grinned triumphantly.

"Anyone could smell that. What else?"

"Uh—tobacco."

"Another lucky guess. That only proves you have a good nose, even though, I must admit, it is the ugliest nose I have ever seen. It's a nose any water buffalo would be proud of, however."

The boy's grin turned into a scowl and his bare feet kicked Loi's shins ferociously.

"Hey, little rabbit-thief. That's what you are . . . like a rabbit trying to steal my cabbages and kicking when you're caught. But kicks won't help you today." Loi grabbed for the sack, but the boy stuffed it inside his shabby shirt and twisted free. He bolted down the street.

With a silent curse, Loi struck out after him again, only to lose him when he vanished around a corner. For a few minutes she searched in vain for his orange hair. Her heart was starting to ache with anguish, when she heard his familiar screams.

"Help! Murder! Murder!"

With a smile, Loi plowed her way through the crowd in the direction of the noise. She stumbled to a halt in front of a small man with close-set, mean eyes who was wearing a tan uniform with red epaulettes. His air of authority made the warning from the old man on the bus suddenly ring in her ears, and she stepped back. But her eyes remained fixed on the sack swinging in the officer's left hand. In his other hand, the boy-thief swung at the air and cursed with words Loi had never imagined. When the boy saw her, he stopped struggling and waved her over.

"Sister, sister, come quickly. This policeman thinks I stole this bag. Tell him the truth."

"Is this your brother's sack, *con-lai?*"

A shiver ran through Loi's body at the insult, but she nodded.

"Ha! I think you both stole it. Can you prove it's yours?" The angry scowl on the policeman's face prevented Loi from speaking.

"Yes, she can prove it. Go ahead, sister, tell him what's inside the bag. Remember, rice, tobacco . . ."

"A little carving. And a photograph of my American father."

The uniformed man opened the bag, unwrapped the blue cloth, and took out the photograph. A wicked smile curled on his lips as he looked at it, then he spat into the street. He shoved the picture back into the bag and rummaged until he found the opened pack of cigarettes. He casually shook out a handful, then tossed the bag at Loi's feet.

"Stay away from here, you fatherless thieves. Go back to your whore mother or I'll throw you in jail and send you off to reeducation camp." He stomped his foot, as if chasing away a mongrel cur, and the boy ran.

Loi picked up the sack and ran toward the steeple —the only place she felt safe. When she finally stopped, she took out the pack of cigarettes and counted them—only ten left. With a sigh, she dropped to the soft green grass and leaned against the eucalyptus tree again. She removed the photo and studied the tall man with the smiling face and curly hair, standing beside her short mother.

"Why did you come here?" she whispered. "My mother was so happy before you came. If you had left her alone, I wouldn't be here now, sitting under a tree with no home."

"Is that really your American father?"

Loi looked up at the orange-haired boy standing very quietly behind her.

"What do you care who this is?" she muttered and rewrapped it carefully. This time she tucked it inside the pocket sewn to the inside of her waist-band.

"My father was American, too," he said with a shrug, then squatted down beside her.

Loi scrutinized his shamelessly ugly face. The broad nose looked more like it belonged to a *moi* tribesman. And the spots on it did not look natural, like her freckles. They were smeared and uneven, as if painted on. His hair, orange and frizzy, was the most unhuman hair she had ever seen. She couldn't imagine how it had ended up in such a condition, but she knew he could not have been born with that hair, for the roots were very black.

"You don't look part American," she finally replied.

"Well, I am," he insisted and stuck his chin out. "Where do you think I got this brown hair and freckled nose?"

"I think you got the freckles from a paintbrush. And only heaven can say how your hair got to be such an awful color of streaked orange."

"Brown! My hair is brown! And curly, like yours."

"All right, all right. Say what you wish. But that still doesn't give you the right to steal my pouch. All I own is inside here."

The boy cocked his head a moment, studying her from under half-closed eyes. Then he grinned and thrust out his hand. Loi stared at it in amazement.

What did he expect her to do with the grime-covered thing?

"*Gimme five,*" he said in English.

"What did you say?"

"It's what they say in America. It means, 'Shake my hand.' "

"Why would I want to touch your filthy hand?"

"Don't act like a stupid country girl. That's what Americans do when they meet somebody. They shake hands. Come on, *gimme five.*"

Loi gingerly reached out and touched the boy's fingers, then quickly withdrew her hand in repulsion.

"What's your name, farm girl?"

"Pham Thi Loi."

"Miss Loi! What an old-fashioned name. Sounds just like something a farm girl would have."

Loi jumped to her feet.

"I was not born on a farm. My mother lived in a big city when I was born. Da Nang. My name is just as good as yours. What is your name anyway, city thief-boy?"

"Joe. Just call me Joe."

"What kind of crazy name is that? It sounds Chinese."

"Don't you know anything about America, girl? Joe is the number-one name for boys. Everybody calls everybody Joe."

"And how do you know so much about America?"

"I told you, my father was American."

"Ha! My mother told me all the Americans left when I was a baby. You're only about twelve years old, the same age as my cousin Dinh. You couldn't have an American father."

"That's what many people say. But my story is unusual."

Loi shook her head. "*You* are unusual, Mr. Joe. Can you tell me the directions to the Foreign Office?"

"You're going to register to go to America?" His dark eyes lit up, and he leapt to his feet.

"Yes. I was on my way there when a certain little thief-boy stole my food sack and got me all turned around in this too-big city. Now I don't know which way to go."

"Don't worry," Joe said as he put his hand on her back and began to steer her across the park. "I know everything there is to know about the Foreign Office and going to America. I'm going, too, you know."

Loi raised one eyebrow.

"You've already registered?" she asked.

"Well . . . not exactly," he said as they began slowly walking down a tree-lined avenue, dodging bicycles. "You see, no one in the Office believes that I'm really half American. It's because I'm so young, you know. But my story is unusual. I keep telling them my father was an *M-I-A*—"

"What is an *M-I-A?*"

"A soldier that got lost and never made it back to

137

America when everybody else left. You see, my father lived in the jungle many years. My lovely mother found him bitten by a snake and sucked the poison from his leg. Then she took care of him in her little hut at the foot of the mountain."

"What kind of snake?"

"A . . . a python, I think it was called."

"Oh, Joe. Pythons aren't poisonous. They wrap themselves around their prey and crush the bones. My uncle caught one once by biting its tail. That makes it let go and . . ."

"Let me finish my story! Who cares what kind of snake it was! Then she took care of him, and he fell in love with her. After I was born and a few years old, one day he said to her, 'I can't live in this jungle anymore. I miss America. I miss *baseball*—' "

"*Baseball?* What is—"

"Shhh! I miss *hotdog* and *John Wayne* movie and *Madonna* tapes. Sorry, beautiful lady of the jungle and handsome little baby boy, but I have got to get back to my wife and three kids."

"What?"

"So my mother, being like an angel, said, 'I love you so much, I will sacrifice my own happiness and help you get back to America.' And she sewed up a skirt and shirt like a Black Thai tribesman's and painted his face brown and walked with him all the way to the border of China."

"China! But isn't China almost two thousand miles away?"

"Maybe it was Cambodia. I was just a child. But my lovely mother was so sad and missed him so much that she left me on the doorstep of that big Catholic church over there, then threw herself into the river. But before she died, she said, 'Joe, you go to America and find your father. Tell him I loved him so much I could not live without him.'"

Joe reached up and pretended to wipe away a tear, but Loi saw no sign of water in his eyes.

"Hmmmph! No wonder the Foreign Office doesn't believe that fairy tale. I bet you don't even have a photo or letter or anything proving your father was American, do you?"

"My sweet angel mother put the only photo she had inside her blouse when she dove into the raging river. It washed away on big bubbles."

"I thought you were on the church doorstep." Loi shook her head, then burst into laughter.

"Why are you laughing? Everything is true, believe me. My mother really did throw herself into the Saigon River."

"I don't doubt that. But more likely it was because she saw your ugly face when you were born."

Joe crossed his arms and turned his back. "I thought you were my friend," he said in a quivery voice. Soon he made loud sobs.

Loi felt a twinge of guilt run through her heart. At least he hadn't insulted her for being a *con-lai*. He was the first person she had ever met who *wanted* to be part American.

"Oh, all right. I'm sorry, Joe. It's a wonderful story. And your mother was an angel."

Joe whirled around with a grin on his face and dry eyes.

"Say, why don't you be my sister?" He reached up and put his hand on her shoulder. "We can go to America together. You can tell the Foreign Office that the man in your photo is my father, too."

"I already have a cousin your age. Why should I want a brother, too? Especially one as ugly as you."

Joe halted in his tracks and crossed his arms again. Loi stopped and turned around.

"Well? What's wrong now?"

"I'm not going to show you where the Foreign Office is."

"All right, all right, all right. I'm sorry I called you ugly. You're as handsome as the Jade Emperor's son," she said, but secretly she thought about when the Jade Emperor's son came to earth disguised as an ugly frog.

Joe kept his feet planted and stubbornly shook his orange hair.

"I don't care what you call me. I want to be your

brother. If you don't claim me for a brother, I won't show you where the Foreign Office is."

"I can ask somebody else. Lots of people know where it is."

"Yes, but do they know exactly what to do? Do they know the names of the men in the Office and how to act and every little secret trick? Do you think that you have to fill out only one little form? Country girl, there are so many forms it would make your head swim. Some to send to the Americans in Bangkok, some for here, some for Hanoi. Without me you're gonna have to wait in line for days."

"Days!" Loi looked at his set chin and clenched lips, then shrugged. "All right, come on, little orange-haired brother."

Joe flashed his white grin, then ran up to Loi and thrust out his dirty hand.

"*Gimme five*, big sister!"

10

THE PARK

T H E L I N E had not moved in the past hour. Loi was sure of it. Women and older teenagers with tense, hopeful faces, some clutching battered suitcases, stood silently in line. Occasionally someone would wipe the perspiration that dripped down his or her face or fan themselves with whatever was at hand. The overhead ceiling fan turned as slowly as the line was moving, creating no breeze. And the open windows and door only served to let in swarms of fruit flies that hovered around everyone's sweat-drenched face.

Loi watched Joe, who was standing next to her, repair the brown spots on his nose and cheeks with a soft brown lead pencil.

"That won't do you any good, Joe," a woman behind them said angrily. "Everyone knows you aren't half American. Selfish people like you just make it harder for those of us who really qualify."

"Ha! Look who's talking. Everyone knows that Linh here isn't really your daughter. It was your younger sister who knew the American soldier. She deserted her baby and ran off."

"You're no better than a sewer rat," the woman hissed back and took a swing at Joe. He ducked, but her fingers passed through his orange hair and stood it on end. In front of them, a different woman grabbed Joe's arm and shook it.

"Your father was no more American than I am. Your father was Nguyen Quan, a good-for-nothing gutter snake. He was murdered down in Cho Lon by a fat Chinese gambler who caught him cheating at dice. And you'll end up no better."

"Say what you please, stooped-back old witch. I know that your son isn't half American, either."

"Don't be ridiculous. Just look at him. His eyes are as round as melons."

"They may be round now, but they weren't round last year. Any quack doctor's knife can make slanted eyes round, if his palm is greased with enough money. Your important brother in the Cultural Office gave you the money for that operation."

"That's outrageous! Why would he do such a thing? He's a dedicated Party member and a good government worker."

"Because he knows that if you go to America, you

143

will start sending him all kinds of merchandise he can sell to make a comfortable living. And later, you can even send for his children."

The woman's eyes grew narrow and her long nails cut into Joe's arm. Soon she and the woman behind her were fighting over who would get to hit him next and shake his brains loose. Loi stepped back to avoid the scuffle. She watched them screaming and accusing each other, and all the while she tried to understand why anyone would want to pretend to be half American. All her life she had cursed her American blood, and now suddenly it was what everyone in this small, crowded room wanted more than anything. If she could just somehow pour out her American blood and sell it to them, she would be the happiest girl in the world. Then she and Khai could marry in the village instead of running away to do it.

Loi ran her fingers through her curly hair and leaned back against a metal pole that bisected the line of people. Soon a man in a tan-colored uniform stepped up and the squabbling stopped. He grabbed Joe by the collar and dragged him toward the front door.

"I've told you a thousand times to stay out of here," the guard said as he hurled Joe onto the sidewalk. The boy hit the concrete on his hands and knees with a loud smack.

Loi watched Joe pick himself up, work on his scraped knees a moment, repair his ruffled hair, and then quietly sneak back inside the room through an open window when the guard's back was turned. From a dark corner, he motioned for her to stay in line.

When she finally reached the gray metal desk piled high with papers, Joe tiptoed to her side and whispered, "Get the cigarettes ready."

The man behind the desk wore his black hair short and oiled to a glossy sheen. His round gold-rimmed glasses reflected a slow-turning electric fan that was pointed at his desk, providing him with the only cool spot in the room. Cigarette smoke hovered above his head, and his ashtray spilled over with tiny stubs.

Joe pushed Loi aside and shoved his hand toward the clerk.

"Mr. Phuoc. *Long time no see.*"

The man glared at Joe. He shook his head, snuffed out his cigarette, and leaned back in his chair with his hands behind his head.

"Not long enough, Joe. What are you trying to get away with this time?"

"No tricks this time. Remember my older sister I told you about a long time ago? The one who lived in Da Nang and who I was trying to get to join me? Well, meet my sister, Miss Loi. *Give Mr. Phuoc five.*"

Loi hadn't gotten used to the idea of a stranger touching her hand, but at least Mr. Phuoc's hands looked clean and Joe seemed to know what he was doing, so she cautiously extended her hand. The man shook it once, briefly, and sat back up.

"So, you're Joe's sister, huh?"

Loi glanced at Joe, saw him wink and make a little signal with his hand. She nodded.

"You say your father is American? Do you have his name and address?"

Loi opened the pouch and retrieved the photograph. She carefully unwrapped it and handed it to the man.

"This is all I have. I don't know his name or address. I think my mother met him in Da Nang."

"You think? You mean you don't even know where you were born?"

Loi hung her head. "I'm not sure."

"Is your mother dead?"

"No."

"Then why isn't she here with you?"

Loi swallowed hard and started to speak up, but Joe jumped in.

"Our mother is very, very sick, Mr. Phuoc. She was not able to travel, but she wants her children to go to America and send for her later, when she gets well. What a wonderful, sacrificing mother she is."

Mr. Phuoc snorted, then chuckled.

"Last month you said your mother died of typhoid fever. You think I'm so stupid that I don't remember these things?" He tapped the side of his head with his index finger.

"No, no, Mr. Phuoc. You must have me confused with some other kid. Not Joe. Joe's mother is sick."

"I don't see you in this photograph, Joe. You're lying again."

"Of course not. I was born later. Just look at this honest country girl, here—my sweet older sister. You know she's not lying."

"I thought you said she came from Da Nang."

"Only born there. Lately she's been working on a farm." Joe slipped one cigarette onto the pile of papers in front of Phuoc. The man ignored it and continued studying the photograph, then scrutinized Loi's face. Joe laid two more cigarettes next to the first one. Mr. Phuoc took one, lit it up, then opened his desk drawer and swept the other two inside, where they landed beside dozens of other cigarettes of all brands and an assortment of watches and jewelry.

"Are you married, Miss Loi?"

"No, not yet. I'm waiting for a boy to join me soon. We got separated on the bus from Da Lat."

"Ah. And is he also Amerasian?"

Loi hesitated a moment. She was sure that Raymond Smith had said spouses of Amerasians could go to America also. She took a deep breath and decided that the truth would be best.

"No, he's not Amerasian. Does that make a difference? He will be able to come, too, won't he?"

"Yes, yes, of course. You're allowed to take your spouse and children. No problem there."

Loi let her breath out slowly. At least there was one less thing to worry about.

"Okay," Mr. Phuoc finally said. "You look Amerasian and the woman in this photo certainly looks a lot like you, so I'm going to approve your request."

Loi closed her eyes a moment and gave a silent prayer of thanks.

Joe grinned as he leaned across the desk, grabbed Phuoc's hand, and pumped it.

"Ten thousand, thousand thanks, Mr. Phuoc. You're the nicest man in all the Foreign Office. We'll send you lots of blue jeans from America."

Phuoc scribbled his illegible signature on the paper in front of him, then stamped it with loud thumps before looking up.

"I didn't say *you* were approved, Joe. Everybody knows you're not Amerasian. I don't want to warn you again about pestering us. I've told you before, if you can find a sponsor in America who will pay for your airplane and exit visa expenses, that's all right with us. I'd be the happiest guy in Ho Chi Minh City to see you on the plane. I'd celebrate all week. Now, get out of here before I have to call the guard."

Phuoc opened a drawer and began pulling out forms.

"It is not a simple process," he said to Loi. "You must fill out this application for the U.S. Orderly

Departure Program office in Bangkok, Thailand. And these papers are for your Letter of Introduction, which must be approved by the Foreign Interest Section here in Ho Chi Minh City, then by the Ministry of Foreign Affairs in Hanoi."

"But I don't know how to . . ." Loi started to say that she didn't know how to read and write very well, but Joe's sharp elbow in her rib cage stopped her. Joe shook his head.

"If Hanoi approves you," Phuoc continued, "your name will be posted on that wall over there. Then I will arrange for a person-to-person interview with an American from the ODP Bangkok office."

"You mean I must travel to Thailand?"

"No, no, no. The Americans come here a few times a year. But you will have to go to Tan Son Nhut Airport on the outskirts of town for the interview. If they approve you, there is a medical exam you must pass."

"No problem," Joe interjected. "My sister is a strong, healthy girl. I've seen her lift a baby water buffalo with one arm."

Phuoc chuckled, then lit up another cigarette. Two thin streams of smoke shot out of his nostrils like dragon's smoke.

"It's up to the Intergovernmental Committee for Migration to interpret the results of your exam. After that, there are still a few more papers to fill out for the Vietnamese Emigration authorities. And of course, you will need an exit visa. The United States will pay for all these applications; however, you will be expected to pay them back after settling in America."

Loi sighed. Raymond Smith had not told her how complicated the process would be. She studied the forms and saw dozens of words that she did not understand.

"How long does all this take?" she asked.

Phuoc shrugged. "Depends. Maybe six, seven, eight months . . . maybe longer."

"What Mr. Phuoc means is that if you have no money to bribe the authorities it may take years," Joe said. "Those with money can get out within the year."

Phuoc's face reddened and he shouted to the guard at the front door. Joe dashed across the room and dove out the open window before the guard moved. Phuoc muttered under his breath, then wrote a number on a card. Loi had not learned to count that high.

"This is your case number. Keep it at all times. Use it on all the papers you fill out." He dismissed her with a wave of his hand, and the light danced off the rim of his heavy gold watch. "Next!" he shouted.

Outside in the bright sunlight, Loi stared at the purple ink drying on the card. Several people in the line that trailed out the front doors glared at her enviously, and she quickly put the card and her photograph into her secret pocket.

At first Loi didn't see Joe, then she heard him cursing and kicking the dirt. This time the tears in his eyes were genuine, and she wanted to hold him in her arms and let him cry on her shoulder. But when she approached him, he rubbed his eyes and stuck his chin out.

"I'm not giving up yet. I'm still going to America, if it's the last thing I ever do. Who needs Mr. Phuoc? I'll just stow away on the airplane inside your suitcase. Right, sister?"

Loi forced a smile for him, then looked at the papers in her hand. "Do you know how to read and write, Joe?"

"No. But I know a guy who will do it for a small fee."

Joe dragged Loi around to the back side of the Foreign Office, where a young man of about twenty-two was seated on the grass, surrounded by several people. Loi had never seen such dark skin and tightly curled hair. But his eyes were slanted slightly like hers and he spoke perfect Vietnamese.

"Is he a mountain tribesman?" she whispered.

Joe laughed. "No, country girl. He is an Amerasian like you. His father was a black G.I. Bob's been trying to go to America for five years. He's an expert at filling out forms. He speaks English, too. Hey, Bob, *gimme five!*" Joe shouted as he held up his hand and walked up to the dark-skinned man.

It took almost an hour for Bob to fill out all the

forms, and then another two hours waiting in line just to return the papers to Phuoc's assistant. Loi felt exhausted by the time she stepped out of the building.

Joe was waiting for her. He grabbed her hand and pulled her across the street to a park lined with beautiful tall tamarind trees and spotted with dozens of people lying on mats and blankets. At first Loi thought Joe wanted to rest in the park, but soon she recognized some of the faces as the same women and teenagers who had been waiting in line at the Foreign Office.

"What is this?" she asked.

"They call this Amerasian Park."

Joe led Loi between women squatted over three-legged charcoal-burning braziers, stirring rice or noodles in cheap tin pots. A middle-aged woman sat picking the lice from her daughter's hair, while the daughter's baby crawled at her feet. A little boy with a bad eye infection stared at Loi, then scooted behind his pale, sickly mother. When Loi hesitated to step over some sleeping people, Joe pulled her hard toward a plum tree whose old, withered branches swooped down to the ground, forming a cool shade. Under it a frayed rush mat was rolled into a tight cylinder. A page from a magazine—a picture of a Japanese man in a white uniform swinging a bat—was tacked to the tree trunk with wire.

"That is *baseball*," Joe said proudly as he pointed at the page. "And this is where I live. You can stay with me until you leave for America," Joe said as he unfurled the shabby straw mat.

"It's . . . it's nice, Joe," Loi said as she slumped to the mat and leaned against the tree. "You've got the best spot in the camp." She gave Joe half of the rice patties she had been saving, then she stretched out. She hadn't realized how sore and tense her muscles were. Soon she was in a deep sleep.

She was dreaming about her village. It was springtime, and the lotus blossoms were choking the irrigation ditches and the village fish pond. But everyone was weeping—her mother, her uncle, her cousins, and Khai. Loi reached out to touch Khai, but her arms passed right through his, and she turned into a misty puff of dragon's breath and flew away.

Loi sat up with a jolt, thinking only one thought: she had to go to the bus station and look for Khai. But she knew she would not be able to find the depot without the help of Joe. And the shadow of the tree was long and skinny now, indicating that it was evening. There wouldn't be much time before dark settled in.

Loi looked around for Joe and noticed that the camp was now alive with new faces. There were now at least two hundred people—many carrying hand tools—and they looked exhausted from a day of hard labor.

It didn't take Loi long to find Joe. After walking only a few meters, she heard a squabble and some women screaming. When Joe saw Loi, he abandoned his arguing and ran up to her, smiling.

"What was that yelling all about?" she asked.

"Nothing to worry about. I take care of myself. I don't need their boiling pot. I'll take care of you, too, sister. Now, are you ready to go out and make some money?"

"Make money? How? All I know how to do is farm rice."

"Don't worry, I'll teach you."

"All right, but before we go to work, can you show me the bus station? I'm expecting someone from Da Lat."

"Da Lat? No, no, no. It's too late for the bus from Da Lat. It comes early in the morning."

"Are you sure? Couldn't there be a bus during the day?"

Joe shook his head vigorously. "You can check buses tomorrow. Right now we have to earn some money. Are you going to help me or not?" He put his hands on his hips and cocked his head sideways.

"All right, if you promise to show me the bus station tomorrow morning."

"Agreed," Joe said impatiently. "Now, the first thing you have to do is give me all your money and those American cigarettes."

Loi jerked her hand free from his.

"I'm not falling for another trick like that."

"What trick are you talking about, country girl?

I'm going to show you how to make money. Come on." He grabbed her hand again and began walking so fast that Loi had to trot to keep up. Soon they reached a busy street bustling with vendors and workers buying items for their evening meal. Joe spotted one old woman with a wooden tray containing about ten different brands of cigarettes from many different countries—France, Britain, Vietnam, Thailand, and the Soviet Union.

"Quick, give me all your money." Joe held out his hand.

Loi studied his face as he concentrated on the old woman. He wiggled his hand impatiently. "Come on, hurry."

Loi fished out the wad of money and plopped it into his hand.

Joe counted out most of it, returned the rest to her, then strolled up casually to the old woman. Soon the two were in an animated bargaining war. Finally he gave her the money and returned with one fresh box of 555 cigarettes and one empty 555 pack.

"Why did you waste all my money on cigarettes?" she protested.

"Shhh . . . I'm busy now." Joe slipped into an alley and removed from his pocket a piece of a barber's straight-edge razor. He carefully slit the plastic on the first pack and removed several cigarettes and placed them in the empty one.

"Now, give me your cigarettes."

He took the American cigarettes and placed them in the back of each box.

"What are you doing?"

"Everybody likes 555 best. They cost more than American brands," he explained as he shook the two boxes.

"Looks like you're still short some."

"No problem." He broke several cigarettes in two and slipped them into the far back of each box. Then he replaced the plastic wrap expertly.

"Now we've got two boxes of 555s. Let's go."

Loi followed Joe to another street where neatly dressed men sat inside restaurants. Old women brushed the sidewalks off in front of their shops with short-handled brooms. It reminded Loi of the hills near her village. Every few months she and Khai's cousin Huong would gather brush to make brooms. Now Huong was dead, and Loi was begging on the streets of Saigon.

An old woman paused, saw Loi staring at her broom, and swatted her legs angrily.

"Get away, *bui-doi*. You'll bring me bad luck."

As Loi stepped back she bumped into Joe.

"She's wrong," he said. "You're not bad luck, big sister. Look, I sold both packs of cigarettes already. Now we can eat like the emperor's children tonight."

"Maybe we shouldn't spend all our money on food," Loi protested as Joe raced toward the Central Market.

"Why save money when you may not be alive tomorrow to spend it? Money today, eat today, is what I always say."

"Well, of course we need *some* food. But remember it was my money that you spent to buy the cigarettes."

Joe stopped in his tracks and whirled around. "Okay, country girl. You're so smart, you do what you want with the money. I'll go get food some other way." He poked the roll of bills into her cloth bag and swaggered away, ignoring Loi's shouts.

Loi continued down the street alone, wishing it wasn't so late. A lot of the vendors had already closed up for the day. Her stomach rumbled as she examined the stalls of fly-covered fish, pork, beef, and ducks hanging from bamboo frames. Of course, she couldn't afford to buy expensive meat, so she walked on to the vegetable stands, where ripe durians dominated the air. First she bought a bottle of *nuoc mam*, some garlic, rice, and vegetables. Then she remembered Joe's argument in the park and splurged on a small tin pot to cook noodles and rice in. Then she thought about Joe's skinny arms and legs, and how he had helped her inside the Foreign Office, and how he was sharing his home. She sighed and returned to the meat stalls, where she bought the smallest chicken she could find and a little basket of coal. By the time she had finished shopping, most of the money was gone.

As Loi started walking toward Amerasian Park, she heard footsteps behind her, then felt a hand on her shoulder.

"I knew you couldn't resist a cute little guy like me, sister," Joe said as he took some of the food from her arms.

That evening, Loi leaned back against the plum tree and watched Joe devour the food so quickly that pieces hung in the corners of his mouth.

"Slow down, Joe. You're eating like a pig."

"Pigs don't get as hungry as me," he mumbled with his mouth full.

Loi didn't eat much. The rice tasted strange and seemed to still have the flavor of the Mekong Delta mud clinging to its grains. She gave Joe her leftovers, wondering how a boy that small could eat so much food. She wasn't as tired as she had been before her nap, but her feet were covered with dust and her clothes stuck to her sweaty, dirty body. She would have traded her food gladly for the opportunity to bathe in the cool mountain stream near her village.

"Joe, where do we bathe around here?"

"Bathe? You *are* crazy, aren't you. We have to be saving with water and only use it for cooking and drinking. But if you must bathe, we can sneak over to the fountain on Trung Hung Dao Street or use the river. But we would have to be very careful. If the police catch anybody on the streets after curfew, the unlucky one goes to jail and never comes back."

"Even children?"

"Especially children. I'll show you later. But we have to wait until it gets darker. That piece of moon will make it hard to sneak around tonight."

Loi glanced at the moon climbing over the tops of the tamarind trees. It seemed to dominate the sky, even though it was only a quarter. *Têt Trung-thu*, the Mid-Autumn Festival, would be here very soon. Many people still called it the Moon Festival, because the moon looks bigger and closer to the earth at this time of year.

Loi stared up at the moon with its squiggly gray lines that looked like a banyan tree. Her mother used to tell her the story of Chu Cuoi, the poor woodcutter who found a magic banyan tree whose leaves granted immortality. But when his bride dug around the roots, the tree stepped right out of the ground and climbed to heaven, taking Chu Cuoi with it over the mountains, over the seas, and across the celestial skies until it landed on the moon.

Loi had planned to tell the story to her younger cousins again this year, or any other stories they wanted to hear. But now they would have to light their *long-den* lanterns alone and walk through the little village without the guidance of their older cousin. Maybe Dinh would take her place this year, forced to be an adult too soon. Loi wondered if her cousins would be thinking about her when they looked at the moon, just as she thought about them.

Their small, innocent hearts must be breaking, believing that she was drowned. She had not given even Dinh a proper farewell. And what about her Uncle Long and her mother? Surely no other daughter in history had been so cruel to her own mother by pretending to die, and all just to get out of an unpleasant marriage.

Loi tried to blink the tears from her eyes, but it was useless, so she let them fall freely.

She thought about Khai and the expression on his face as he ran after the bus. Then she thought about his brother Quy, arguing in the middle of the road. Maybe he had recognized Loi. If so, he would have told the villagers and Officer Hiep. Maybe her Uncle Long was on his way to reeducation camp at this very moment and her mother and cousins homeless.

A sob rose from Loi's lips as she curled up into a tight ball, pressing her back against Joe's limp sleeping body on the straw mat.

And if Quy had recognized her, then surely he had held Khai back and made him return home. What might have happened then? Did Quy beat him? Was Khai disowned by his family? Maybe they had arranged his marriage to the strange-acting Suong. Or maybe Khai was on top of the bus from Da Lat, thinking of her. It was this final thought Loi clutched at as she drifted off to sleep.

11

THE SELL

THE LAUGHTER of children and the tantalizing aroma of sweet moon cakes surrounded Loi as she stood on Dong Khoi Street, watching brightly colored paper lanterns bob and weave like a crooked parade of fireflies. Small children were singing songs and trying to keep their lanterns from catching on fire as they marched down the street. Many of the children carried paper toys that represented every shape and color imaginable—dragons, tigers, fish, stars, moons—all dangling from the ends of long bamboo poles.

A sudden gust of wind tumbled several lanterns upside down, catching the thin rice paper on fire like elephant grass in the dry season. Little shrieks of anguish blended with the singing as boys and girls stomped out the flames. The more fortunate children were wearing colorful *ao dai*, which rustled in the wind as they steadily moved down the avenue.

Loi shivered as the breeze whipped through her thin blouse, the same one she had been wearing the day she arrived in Saigon almost two weeks before. It was unseasonably cool for September, and the dark clouds that played hide-and-seek with the full harvest moon held the promise of heavy rain. A whirlwind chased leaves down the street and slammed them against the boarded-up walls of the old Continental Hotel, while grotesque shadows of children swayed on the sides of the buildings. Off to her right, Loi heard dance music from an old hotel that had the word "Rex" and a big king's crown on top of it. She saw young laughing couples coming and going. One of the boys was tall and slender, and though he was wearing black slacks and a crisp white shirt, he looked like Khai. Loi stepped closer, holding her breath until the boy passed by, smelling of strong cologne.

Of course it wasn't Khai. She had known that in her mind, but it was her stubborn heart that would not give up. Her heart made her walk to the bus station every morning to watch passengers disembark from the old green DeSoto that came from Da Lat. She had learned the bus schedule, even though it was never on time, and the toothless old driver knew her face.

She had seen the *cyclo* driver Hung several more times waiting for passengers and reading his newspaper. He always spoke to her and he had a friendly smile. He even invited her to eat at his house once, but Loi felt it would be a betrayal to Khai.

Loi sighed as she turned her attention back to the festival parade. She wished Joe was with her, but he had left over an hour ago with a sad face. "I hate the Moon Festival," he had said in a huff before running off. This was strange, Loi had thought, for she had gotten to know him well over the past two weeks and found him to be a boy who made light of every situation and who had a solution for every problem.

Curious to see where the parade would end, Loi followed the procession. It didn't take long for her to figure out where they were headed, for up ahead on the river, more colored lights twinkled as if half the stars had fallen into the black waters. Then she heard the steady pounding of drums and the high-pitched strings of a *ty-ba*. The wind whirled more strongly, speaking in a thousand voices as it rocked a dozen *tam-ban* boats clustered together. The air hitting Loi's face was chilly, so she didn't feel foolish suddenly breaking into a run alongside the small children whose lanterns had already burned up.

Standing on the riverbank, she saw that the lights were not lying on the water but on a large, flat barge where musicians played. Flowers draped the sides of the boat, and in its center was a stage with dancing puppets. Loi watched the puppets and listened to the music until parents led the last of the children off and the barge slowly churned back up the river. By now the moon was high overhead, a small, scarred silver disk, and the wind was rattling the thatch-covered houseboats docked along the wharf.

Joe still had not rejoined her, and Loi felt a deep, terrifying loneliness. Seeing people merrily bustling in and out of shops, which had remained open late for the festivities, only served to make Loi feel more alone.

She stopped in front of a French bakery. Under glass cases, all kinds of strange pastries beckoned her: cream horns, *gâteaux*, napoleons, puff pastries, and long baguettes. The intoxicating aroma pulled her inside, and though her brain told her it was foolish to waste the last of her money on such luxuries, Loi purchased two moon cakes wrapped in pink tissue paper. She ate one, then tucked the other into her cloth pouch.

As she passed a park fountain, she paused to wash off her bare feet and arms. She would have preferred a complete bath, but she could feel eyes staring at her from the dark shadows, and on a corner a policeman watched every move she made. With a shiver, Loi hurried back to Amerasian Park.

She found Joe curled up into a tight ball like a cat on top of the dirty mat. She tapped his shoulder lightly.

"Joe, I brought you something."

He turned his head and saw the moon cake in her hand. He sat up.

"Where did you get the money?"

Loi shrugged. "I had a little hidden away. Here, eat this. It's good. Not as good as my mother used to make, but still very good. And Mrs. Dung lent me two teacups and a little tea. I wish it was jasmine tea, but I'm thankful for her kindness."

Joe ate the moon cake slowly and sipped the tea from a tiny, handleless blue china cup. Loi saw that his eyes were puffy and rimmed with red. He seemed to notice her discovery, for he turned his head while he continued to eat. Then he licked his fingers and sighed. When he faced her again, he smiled.

"Thank you, big sister."

"Do you want to tell me why you were crying? Or should I mind my own business?"

Joe snapped a piece of dead plum tree in his fingers and didn't look her in the face.

"It's a stupid reason."

"Maybe not."

"It's just that every festival reminds me that I have no family. Did you know I've never even owned a *long-den* lantern? I've never walked in a lantern parade."

"Is that why you were so sad tonight?"

He shrugged, then shook his head.

"Not exactly. You see, tonight I found a lantern

in the street, half burned-up but still usable. For the first time in my life I did have a lantern. I was so happy. But when I tried to join in the parade, some older boys laughed at me and shoved me away, saying I was too old to join in. They called me a mother's baby and other insults you wouldn't want to hear."

"I'm sorry, Joe."

"It doesn't matter. I know in my heart they're right. I am too old to take part in children's parades and children's festivals. But I never did those things when I was a child. I feel like a very old man sometimes."

Loi moved behind Joe and wrapped her arms around him, resting her chin on top of his orange hair. "It's all right. Tonight you can be a child and I will be the adult. Would you like for me to tell you some fairy tales? I know so many it would make your head spin. Stories about beautiful fairies, or grand warlords, or simple woodcutters. Any story, just ask."

Joe sighed. "Tell me a story about a boy with no mother and no father who goes to America and becomes happy."

Loi chuckled but saw that Joe was not laughing. He stared across the park, where mothers were rocking their babies to sleep and teenagers were lowering their work-weary bones onto grass mats. A few young men squatted on their heels, playing a game of thirteen-card poker, gambling with cigarettes instead of money. The cool air made everyone huddle close together and speak in low voices.

Loi told Joe the most fantastically wild story she could imagine, though she knew very little about America. Every time she described a town or person, Joe would correct her, and soon he was telling the story in his own words. The lanterns in the camp went out one by one and the gamblers broke up their game. By the time Joe finished his story, the park was silent, save for the whistling wind and the creaking bamboo and the rasping cough of an old man.

"You know, I would give up my whole future days on earth for just one month in San Francisco, USA," Joe said finally, in a matter-of-fact voice. "Don't you feel like that sometimes?"

Loi didn't take her eyes off the tiny silver moon with its eerie blue-gold halo.

"Yes, I do," she said slowly. "Sometimes I feel like I would give up my future days for just one month back in my village with my family and the boy I love."

Joe gave her a strange look, then rolled over and fell into a deep sleep.

The next morning, Joe and Loi awakened with cold drops of rain pelting their heads. They leapt to their feet, rolled up the damp straw mat, and ran to the covered porch of the Foreign Office building. Being the weekend, it was deserted, except for other people seeking refuge from the sudden rain shower.

Loi had given up on going to the Office every day. Each time, the clerk told her not to worry, her name and number would be posted when the time came. But she had feared deeply that she might overlook her name on the list, or that some mistake might be made and her name left off. So she had endured the long line and the angry looks of the guard and the clerk for the first week. But now, all her time was spent trying to find ways to eat.

The rain bombarded the banana leaves like bullets, and the thunder rumbled angrily. Although the cool air felt good after a long summer of searing temperatures and rain was a sign of good luck, no one wanted to see their sleeping place turned into a mud sty. And if the sun came out later, the steam and humidity would smother the city like a blanket. Only the old man standing under the eaves, performing his morning ritual of *tai chi*, seemed oblivious to the rain. He slowly, gracefully, swept his arms to the left, to the right, shifting his weight in a simulated battle with a gentle invisible enemy. Even the sprays of water that splattered against his face did not distract him from his slow-motion battle.

When the rain finally stopped, Loi's rumbling stomach told her it was midmorning. The streets glistened like a freshly washed water buffalo's back, and the smells of jasmine and plumeria drifted on the breeze.

"Do we have any money left?" Joe asked.

"No. I spent the last of it on the moon cakes. I know it was foolish, but you looked so sad last night."

Joe grinned. "We all have bad days, huh? Even Joe America. Let's go find something to eat. I saw Duy's mother boiling up a pot of noodles on the sidewalk."

"I don't think she will let us eat with her again. The last time, she almost hit you with the ladle."

"You're right. That old woman is not right in the head anyway. We're going to have to find some other way to get food today."

"Where are we going?"

"Down to the quay."

"No, Joe. I told you before, it isn't right to steal."

"Well, it isn't right to starve, either," he said without stopping.

"Don't you still carry a bruise on your behind from the last time you tried the river docks?"

"I feel lucky today. My bottom feels hard like a rock. I can stand anything." He slapped his behind and danced a little jig in the middle of the street until Loi laughed out loud.

At the river quay, screaming seagulls dove at fishermen's boats, and workers bustled to and fro loading heavy sacks and crates onto large ships with foreign flags. Joe motioned for Loi to remain silent as they crept closer to a ship being loaded with bulging white sacks. One man oversaw the skinny laborers, each of whom hoisted a bag on his back and almost buckled from the weight. Occasionally the overseer shouted an order as he rocked back on his boot heels, his hands behind his back.

Joe and Loi sneaked behind the old green army transport truck from which the men were unloading the sacks. The driver sat with the door open, smoking a cigarette, his feet propped up.

"Remember what I told you," Joe whispered. "You get the attention of the overseer by the ship. I'll get some rice. Give me your hat."

Loi removed the cone-shaped *non-la*, threw her shoulders back, and casually strolled toward the overseer. His dark eyes raked over her slender figure as she stepped up, smiling her most charming smile and twisting a loose curl of hair.

"Excuse me, sir. I'm looking for the boat just coming in from Hong Kong."

"Hong Kong? I haven't seen any ships from Hong Kong. What is its name?"

"Uh . . . that's the problem, sir. I don't know the name. Only that it is arriving from Hong Kong today. Family of mine is going to be on it. If I can't find the ship, I don't know what I'll do." She pouted her lips and sniffed, but all the while she glanced over the short man's shoulder and watched Joe. He silently removed the piece of razor blade from his pocket, pressed the hat to a sack, then cut a small slice in it. Loi smiled as she saw the thin white line of rice tumble into the hat.

The overseer smiled back at her, then looked at her eyes. Suddenly he whirled around.

"You! Stop! Thief!" he yelled.

Like Joe had taught her, Loi quickly kicked the overseer behind his right knee. He gave a grunt, his leg folded, and he collapsed to the dock. Faster than a rabbit, Loi charged toward Joe. As she passed him, he shoved the hat into her hands and ran in the opposite direction with the truck driver and overseer on his tail.

After pausing long enough to transfer the rice from her hat to the food pouch slung around her neck, Loi hurried to the rendezvous point—a small circular park with a fountain in its center. Joe was already waiting.

"Why didn't you keep his attention longer?" he said angrily. "I hardly got enough rice for one meal this time. Now he knows our faces and won't trust us again."

"I told you it isn't right to steal," Loi said. "Besides, it's too risky."

Joe slammed his palm against the wall of the fountain.

"I'm tired of getting caught all the time. Before you came, I could get what I needed. Didn't take much food for me. Now I work twice as hard for half the food. You bring me bad luck, country girl."

Loi swallowed hard as she hung her head and stared at the dirty street. "You don't have to stay with me. You were the one who wanted me to be your big sister, remember? Go ahead and make a living for yourself. Don't worry about me. I can survive alone," she said in a quavering voice.

"You? You, the dumb country girl? If I leave you alone for one day, you're gonna end up selling your butt to the first rich man who comes along and likes your pretty face."

"I can do a lot of things. I can break big rocks into little ones, like Ty does."

"Ha! Ty's got muscles like an elephant. Look at your skinny arms. Nobody's gonna hire a skinny girl like you to haul those big rocks."

"I can always sell some of my blood."

"You don't have any blood left in those skinny arms, girl. That would make you so sick and weak you'd be no good to anybody."

Loi sighed and plopped down on the edge of the fountain. For the thousandth time she wished she had never left her village.

"Look, country girl, don't worry. I just thought of something we can do. Come on." Joe grabbed her hand and began walking at a fast pace.

Loi followed Joe toward a part of town she had

never seen before. The shops here didn't glisten with shiny imports from Japan or Thailand. There were no sweet-smelling French bakeries or sidewalk cafés where men in clean white shirts sipped glasses of *ca-phe da* and ate noodle soup for breakfast. Here, the smell of waste and garbage choked the air and broken shop windows had been boarded up. Beggars seemed to outnumber the pedestrians and ragged children moved about in gangs.

As they walked passed one building, the door opened and a pale, skeletonlike old man with a wispy white beard stumbled out in a cloud of strange-smelling smoke. His yellowed eyes stared at Joe a moment without seeing, then he wandered across the street and squatted inside another smoky door.

Joe looked at Loi, then shook his head.

"A poppy-eater. Poor old devil. I bet he's up to a hundred fifty smokes a day by now."

"Do you know that old man?"

Joe stared across the street a long time before answering.

"I used to know him before the opium claimed his soul. Now, nobody knows him."

They walked a bit farther, then Joe stopped and turned to face Loi. He pointed at a sign that said White Tiger Street.

"Listen, country girl. I know you're not stupid, but don't ever come here alone. Never. I'm scared

173

silly being here right now in the daylight. At night, you might as well commit suicide as come here. You gotta be crazy, desperate, to come here."

When Joe started to walk again, Loi took his arm and pulled him back.

"Wait, Joe. Why are we here? We're not that desperate, are we? We've got enough food for one day. I still have one thing I can sell. I didn't want to but . . ."

Loi reached inside her bag and removed the teakwood carving of the water buffalo that Khai had given her. Her fingers stroked the curved back and ridged horns as if it were a beloved family pet.

"I love this little buffalo so much. It's all I have left of Khai."

"That's the boy you were engaged to, right?"

Loi nodded, unable to speak. She didn't want to admit that Khai was never coming to Saigon. As long as she didn't say the words out loud, maybe they wouldn't be true. She suddenly thought about the bus schedule. Today was the first day in two weeks she had not checked the bus station. She told herself it was because of the heavy rain, but still a sharp lump rose to her throat.

"Put the little carving back, sister. Maybe you won't have to sell it yet. Let me try one thing here. If this doesn't work, you can sell the buffalo."

Loi wiped her eyes and nodded. "All right. We'll just try one thing here."

Farther down the street, Joe stopped beside a big pothole where rain had collected. He dipped the corner of his shirt in it, then wiped the dirt and smudges from Loi's face and told her to wash off her bare feet.

"You've gotta look clean and pretty. Pull your hair back and braid it. And take your hat off."

Loi did as instructed, wondering what he had in mind this time. Joe plucked a pink oleander blossom that peeked through a crack in a bamboo fence, then pushed it into Loi's hair.

"Now, you don't have to do or say anything. Just stand here. When I look in your direction and wave, you smile real big and pretty."

"Joe . . . what are you trying to do?"

"Don't worry. I know what I'm doing. I've done this before. When you see me walking toward you with a gentleman, you smile and wave and step back into this alley. Then you run like crazy to the other end and back toward our regular rendezvous spot. I'll catch up with you later."

Loi stood in the entrance of a bleak little side street that smelled of urine and garbage. The recent rain had left it wet, and she could feel mud oozing between her bare toes. Loi's pulse quickened as she watched Joe walk haughtily down the street toward a crumbling four-story building where women and girls stood. Loi had never seen women wear such short skirts and low-cut, revealing blouses. Even from this distance she could see their red lips and powdered faces. They glared at Joe. Some cursed him. Others mocked and heckled him, but he stood his ground.

When two *cyclos* drove up, each containing a well-dressed gentleman, Joe's voice got all squeaky like it did when he was pretending to be angry. The women slapped at Joe and punched at him, but he pointed toward Loi and waved. Loi waved back and forced a smile. Her pulse was so loud in her eardrums that she couldn't hear Joe's voice.

One of the gentlemen walked off with the leader of the girls and the other man began walking toward the alley with Joe. Loi was sure her knees would buckle from the shaking, but she smiled and waved and slowly stepped back into the alley just as the man approached. She could hear Joe now, chattering like a raven.

"This girl is from the country, all fresh. She's never even talked to a grown man before. I guarantee you're the first. Wait till you see her beautiful face. It's as smooth as a lotus blossom."

Loi disappeared into the alley, and faster than the wind, her feet flew over the slippery mud. She heard the man's angry shouts and Joe's squeals but dared not look behind her. As she slowed for the corner, she felt a sharp pain in her left foot but staggered on. As she burst into the sunlight, she saw three teenage boys rummaging in a pile of junk. Their dirty faces showed white grins as they came toward her.

"Look here, what luck. We've been hunting for

something to eat, but this is much, much better," one of them said and reached for Loi's arm.

She stepped back and felt a jab of pain in her foot again. She glanced down and saw blood trickling onto the grass.

"Come here, pretty one," another boy said and began to circle to the other side.

"No, leave me alone," she screamed, then kicked the nearest boy with all her strength on his kneecap. With a groan he fell to the ground. Loi ran again, this time not stopping to look at the wound on her foot until she had safely reached the familiar rendez-vous spot at the fountain.

Tears of pain stung her eyes as she lifted her foot and looked at the ugly piece of jagged glass protruding from it. With her eyes closed and her teeth gritted, she jerked it out. She pressed her thumb against the wound, but blood gushed out and dripped down her hand. She dipped her foot into the pool, and soon the water turned pink. But the bleeding would not stop. With a sigh of anger, Loi dug into the secret pocket inside her waistband and withdrew the photo of her American father wrapped in the faded piece of blue *ao dai*.

She removed the piece of silk and wound it tightly around her foot. She stared a moment at the photo of the smiling soldier and the sweet expression on her mother's face, then she drew in a deep, long breath and gently put it back in her pocket. When she looked down, the blue cloth was soaked with blood, but the flow had stopped.

Loi waited half an hour, wondering if maybe she had misunderstood Joe's instructions. They had more than one meeting place, but she was sure this was the one he had meant. After an hour, the gnawing pain in her stomach was so strong and the growling noises so loud that she nibbled a few of the raw grains of rice from the cloth pouch.

Another hour passed and Loi reluctantly began the long walk back to Amerasian Park. She might as well go ahead and cook the rice and have it ready for Joe when he came back. Probably he had found another scheme to get money, or better still, he was spending all the cash he had swindled from the gentleman in the alley. He might even be waiting for her back at the park. She wondered how much money he had gotten.

It was not quite the same as stealing. After all, a man who was going to pay for the use of a girl's body wasn't a very nice person. It wasn't the same as stealing from some poor old woman who needed the money.

Loi limped across the street, lost in thought. As she took a shortcut through a small bamboo grove, she heard a noise and stopped. Someone was lying on the ground—probably a drunk. Then she saw a familiar shabby blue shirt and orange hair.

"Joe!"

She ran to his side and dropped to her knees. Even before she turned him over, she saw the red bloodstains soaked into the dirt and smeared on the leaves of the bamboo plants. As she rolled him over gently, tears welled up in her eyes.

"Oh, my dear, sweet brother Joe."

She had to guess that it was Joe, for the face was so beaten and covered with blood that it was not recognizable. She pulled him close and wiped off what blood she could, but the orange hair was already matted with dark clots.

Loi scooped him into her arms and half ran, half limped toward the fountain one block away. She laid him gently on the cobblestone border and dipped his shirt into the water over and over until she had cleaned all his wounds. Then she rinsed his shirt and scooped him up again. As she started to cross the street, a *cyclo* squealed to a stop in front of her.

"Well, well, little country girl. I see you're still alive," the *cyclo* driver said. Loi looked up into the familiar twinkling eyes of the driver named Hung. When he saw Joe's face, he frowned and shook his head.

"Poor kid. Somebody you know?"

"My brother. Please, can you take us to Amerasian Park? I can't pay you now, but I will have some money later."

The *cyclo* driver studied her face, then nodded. "Put him in the seat. But that boy needs some medicine or he's going to be scarred up very bad."

"Do you know where I can get some medicine?"

"Yes. I know a Chinese herbalist over in Cho Lon, but it will cost a lot."

Loi looked at Joe's face as she climbed in beside him and held his limp hand in hers.

"How will you get the money to pay the doctor?" Hung asked as he steadied himself, then pushed off the curb and began pedaling as fast as he could into the traffic.

Loi didn't answer for a long time because she didn't want her lips to say the words. When she spoke, it was hardly more than a whisper.

"Never mind where the money will come from. I know how to get it now."

I 2

THE CHOICE

FIFTEEN MINUTES after leaving the Chinese herbalist's office in Cho Lon, Loi's nose still stung from the sharp odor of herbs and roots and jars of foul-smelling concoctions that had been fermenting for years.

But Joe was sleeping peacefully now on the padded seat of the *cyclo*, and his fever had gone down. Soon Hung was pedaling down Nguyen Hue Street, where thousands of fresh-cut flowers soaking in buckets of water lined the sidewalks and street. The big white, pink, and red dahlias reminded Loi of the little village school yard where the students worked every day tending the flower beds and jujube orchard to earn money for school supplies. She wished her little cousin Hoa could see this street. Hoa's skinny legs and arms would fly as she dashed in and out of the stalls, laughing and sniffing each bouquet like a honeybee.

"I think your orange-haired brother is going to be all right," Hung said, cutting into Loi's thoughts.

"I pray his face won't be too scarred."

"I agree. It's already ugly enough to stop a clock."

Loi glanced over her shoulder at the smiling face of the driver. He had been much more helpful than she had imagined, and she could not quite understand why he was being so kind to her, a simple "country girl." But he had helped her carry Joe inside the herbalist's room and had argued with the plump Chinese man there, who at first refused to interrupt his mahjongg game. But Hung had insisted and carried Joe right inside and laid him on a cot. Then he did something that caught Loi by surprise. He reached into his pocket and took out a roll of bills and told the Chinese man he would pay for the medicine. Loi was sure the man overcharged them and knew they would have gotten a better price if he hadn't seen the money first. But what was done was done. Joe was alive and safe, and now her only worry was how to get the money to repay the driver.

A jarring bump over a pothole brought Loi out of her daydream. When she looked up she saw the silhouette of the Foreign Office and the trees that lined Amerasian Park. After he had carried Joe to the plum tree and laid him gently on the straw mat, Hung removed his own hat and ran his arm over his damp brow. His dark eyes swept over the groups of scraggly people huddled on the ground under trees and beneath makeshift roofs of bamboo and banana or palm leaves.

"How long have you been living here?" he asked.

"Since the day I arrived. About two weeks."

He shook his head as he looked at her face. He twirled his hat in his hands a moment, looking at the ground.

"How is your foot?"

"It will be all right. I'll wash it every day in clean water. I've had worse cuts. Hung . . . I will repay you as soon as I can. Where will I be able to find you when I get the money?"

"I usually stop at that fountain at noon to wash my face. I'm not hard to find. Just ask any of the *cyclo* drivers on Dong Khoi Street."

As he turned to go, Loi called out.

"Hung, your kindness for saving Joe's life will be rewarded by the gods."

He shrugged. "I didn't exactly do it for Joe." He replaced his cap, climbed onto the bicycle, and shoved off.

Loi stayed by Joe's side the rest of the day, sprinkling the crushed herbal powder over his wounds. Then she boiled the rice they had stolen and made a thin rice soup, which she spooned into Joe's mouth when he awakened. He mumbled something about three teenage boys beating him up and stealing his money, then closed his eyes and drifted back to sleep.

The night air was cool again and distant thunder and small flashes of lightning promised to deliver more rain in the early-morning hours. Rumors flew through the park until everyone knew that Joe had been beaten up. Although most of the residents considered Joe a pure nuisance, Mrs. Dung loaned Loi an old blanket to cover Joe's shivering body and Mrs. Anh gave Loi a little bit of fish to put into the rice soup.

Luckily the rain held back its fury and turned into a gentle drizzle that beaded up in Joe's hair. When he woke at dawn, he ate the rest of the soup and asked Loi what had happened. After listening to Loi's explanation, Joe smiled weakly, thanked her, and closed his eyes again.

After dribbling the last of the herbal medicine onto Joe's wounds, Loi knew she would have to go out and find food alone. The thought of trying to survive without Joe made her heart pound. She didn't know where to begin, so she went to the bus station. As usual, the green DeSoto unloaded its passengers from Da Lat without any sign of Khai's familiar slender body.

After that, Loi checked all the usual places for food scraps, but few people were out because of the light rain. As the morning dragged on, a deep sense of futility settled over Loi. Without Joe, she felt as lost as an unwanted mongrel dog. She was just an inexperienced farm girl, who knew nothing but rice planting and tending and harvesting. She could swing baskets of water from the irrigation ditch to the rice paddy faster than any other girl in her village; she could catch rabbits bare-handed; she could shinny up a banyan tree; she knew where the juiciest mangoes grew. But what good did all those skills do her in this city of four million?

Orphans and other Amerasians worked the streets, often in gangs, begging, scheming, tricking, or out-and-out stealing from people. But Loi didn't want to be like them—the homeless dust of life floating about with no future. And she wasn't like them. She was just waiting. Soon she would be in America—in a clean home with lots of clothes and food, working as a clerk in a store. At least, that was what Joe kept telling her.

Pausing in front of a shop to remove her *non-la* covered with beads of rainwater, she caught her reflection in the glass. The shabby blouse torn at the elbows, the dirty, baggy pants, and the matted hair startled her. For a moment she thought she was looking at one of the beggars. Loi reached up and touched her cheek to make sure it was really her face staring through the layers of dirt and grime.

Angry at herself for looking so beastly and angry

at Joe for having gotten them into such a predicament, she found a pool of water on the sidewalk and scrubbed her face so hard that it turned rosy pink.

All the while Loi walked down the streets, not sure what she was looking for, a thought kept nagging at the back of her mind, and she kept pushing it back again and again. Once she looked up and almost jumped when she recognized White Tiger Street and the same alley where she had cut her foot the day before.

Quickly she turned around and ran until her foot throbbed and she could go no farther.

"How could I even think of doing such a thing?" she said in a loud, firm voice. "I would rather starve than sell my body."

By late morning, the pain in her foot was constant and her stomach screamed. Weakness flooded over her body, making her knees tremble with each step she took. But every place she looked for food turned up empty. She tried the river docks again, but the overseer immediately recognized her and chased her away, shouting for the police.

"What am I going to do?" Loi said to the air, after she stumbled over a sudden rise in the ground and landed on her palms with a smack. She sat there for a moment, too tired and weak to get up. Then she dragged herself to her feet again. She wondered if Joe had awakened yet and if his fever was gone. He would probably be hungry and weak and waiting for her to bring back some food.

With a sigh, Loi resumed her search, pushing thoughts of White Tiger Street out of her mind. But like a rat creeping back to a pile of garbage, her thoughts kept returning to it. And Loi smelled that part of town—like a pile of garbage—before she rounded the corner and saw the familiar alley again.

"I will only do this one time, to repay the *cyclo* driver and to get some food for Joe," she said out loud to bolster her courage. She had the plan in her mind already. She would not let anyone touch her. She would trick them into paying her first, then run away, just as Joe had planned yesterday. But what if she couldn't run fast enough on her sore foot? What if the man shouted and called her terrible names and everyone knew what she had been trying to do? And worst of all, what if the man caught her? Loi stopped and leaned on a street lamp to keep her shaky knees from collapsing. Her heart pounded and told her to turn back, but soon her feet were moving again.

The same girls and women who had strolled the street yesterday were out. Only the bossy one had an umbrella; the others huddled under awnings and eaves, stepping out only when a certain kind of gentleman walked down the street or arrived in a *cyclo*. The old man she had seen leaving the opium house the day before still squatted on his heels across the street in the same place she had last seen him.

When a middle-aged man stopped in front of the women, Loi watched the girl with the umbrella walk up to him, loop her arm through his, and vanish up the stairs of the streaked white stucco building. An upstairs window flew open and loud American rock-and-roll music blared out. In the background a baby wailed. A few minutes later, the music stopped and the man emerged and continued down the street. Shortly after that, the girl with the umbrella returned and assumed her corner of the street.

As a large, black Russian-made car crept down the street, the girls scampered to the edge of the curb and began prancing. Their legs, exposed beneath tight miniskirts, glistened with rain, and their high heels clicked on the concrete. But the car continued to inch slowly past them toward Loi. The bossy girl with the umbrella rushed ahead of the car. Her face was covered with a thick layer of makeup and her eyes were outlined with black. The lips that cursed Loi were the deep shade of ripe plums. Loi had heard of lipstick and had seen it in the shop windows, but she had never been so close to a woman wearing it. The girl's perfume, a heady mixture of jasmine and orange blossoms, stung Loi's nostrils.

"Get outta here, farm girl. Go back to the rice paddies. You don't belong here. Get out." The girl stomped her small foot and sliced the air with long red fingernails as she gestured. But when the black automobile stopped, the girl flashed a big white smile and leaned over toward the passenger in the back-seat.

"Hey, Mr. Dao, you remember me? Best time you ever had. Good price. Good job. Number one."

The man's dark eyes, like chips of black stone set in the side of a rock cliff, didn't blink.

"You," he said, pointing to Loi.

But the umbrella girl stepped in front of Loi and pushed her aside. "Hey, you don't want this one, Mr. Dao. She's a farm girl. Smells like pigs and water buffaloes. She don't know how to treat a man. She's number-ten girl."

The man reached into his pocket, counted out a few large bills, and handed them to the bossy girl.

"Clean her up and bring her to my place in fifteen minutes. You know where it is. Don't be late."

"You're okay, Mr. Dao. Don't worry, I'll take care of this little honeybee."

As the car sped off, the girl in the high heels stuffed the roll of bills into her low-cut top and reached for Loi.

"Come on, pig girl. Maybe you're good for something after all."

Loi stepped back, away from the red nails scraping her arm.

"I-I've changed my mind," she stuttered.

"I said come on. Hurry. You've been bought. Mr.

Dao is a very important man. Big government official. If he likes you, maybe he'll buy you a dress like mine. You won't have to worry about eating for a long time. He's kinda strange but has lots of money. I'll help you find customers, and you give me half the money from now on. Pretty soon, you'll be number-one girl like me."

Loi twisted her arm free of the clasping red nails.

"I don't want to be like you. I just need money this one time."

The umbrella girl tilted her head to one side and laughed.

"Sure, sure. Just one time. That's the same thing I said ten years ago, when I was fourteen years old. 'Just one time, so I can feed my baby.' "

"You had a baby?" Loi said in surprise.

"Sure. Lots of babies since then, too. Now, come on. Mr. Dao gets mad when he has to wait. He won't ask for you again if you don't act right."

The red nails dug into Loi's arm again, making her flesh creep. She had not even thought about becoming pregnant. Khai would never marry her then. No man would marry her. With a sudden lurch, Loi jerked free, feeling the sharp nails leave a long trail down her arm.

"No! I can't do it! I can't!" she yelled and began to run. Even at the end of White Tiger Street, Loi could still hear the umbrella girl cursing and the clicking of high heels chasing her.

By the time Loi arrived back at the water fountain in the clean part of town, her left foot was throbbing out of control and she felt a sticky wetness. She knew the wound had reopened, but there was nothing she could do, so she kept on walking. The drizzle had stopped and men in white shirts sat around sidewalk tables sipping beer or *ca-phe da* and eating bowls of *pho* and French sandwiches. Loi sat on a curb to catch her wind a moment and breathed in the aroma of hot food. Most of the people at the tables gave her angry scowls, but one young man threw a piece of sandwich roll at her feet.

Loi picked up the crusty, hard roll. A little pâté and a single cilantro leaf still clung to part of it. Although her stomach screamed for her to eat like an animal, she took small bites and ate slowly. When she stood, a spot of blood stained the sidewalk where her foot had rested. Now the pain was stronger than ever and had moved up her leg. She tried not to touch the ground with the heel of her foot as she limped away.

Slowly Loi walked up and down the streets, pausing to lean on street lamps from time to time. Finally, the pain would let her go no farther. She sat on the curb of a street burgeoning with dozens of merchant shops. While she rested, she heard a gang of children chanting.

"Lien-xo! Lien-xo!" they said over and over, as they fell in step behind some white-skinned tourists.

Large-boned, overweight, and wearing clothes that seemed too hot and bulky, the tourists ignored the children. The three men and two women stopped outside several shops, sometimes going inside for only a few minutes, usually not buying. Loi stepped closer, hoping to get a better look.

"Are they Americans?" Loi asked a girl next to her.

"No. *Xo-Viet*—Soviets. You should see how much they eat." The girl puffed her cheeks full of air until she looked like a fat hog, then giggled. "But they don't buy anything. They're cheap-pockets. They look here and there and everywhere. Point and mumble—jabber, jabber, jabber. But they don't reach into their cheap pockets. They don't give us candy or money, no matter how cute and pitiful we look." The little girl sighed and put her frail chin on her skinny knuckles.

"Too bad," Loi said as she joined the crowd following the Russians. She studied the strange yellow hair and blue eyes of one of the women and the rolls of fat on her stomach. She imagined they must be richer than emperors to be able to eat so much food. One of the women stopped in front of a shop and pointed at something. She spoke a few words and smiled. Loi followed the short, chunky finger.

"Oh!" Loi sucked in her breath and put her hand over her mouth. She broke into a smile and tears filled her eyes as she stared at a teakwood carving of a water buffalo exactly like the one she carried in her pocket. The only difference was that the one in the window had a streak of lighter wood running down its face. There were a couple more carvings next to it, all similar.

"Khai! I don't believe it! Khai has been here," she whispered.

Not even considering the Russians, Loi squeezed between the hefty bodies and rushed into the shop. She lifted the figurine from the display and turned it over. Just as she expected, there were no craftsman's initials on the bottom. Tears spilled over the brims of her eyes as she squeezed them tightly and pressed the little buffalo to her chest. She touched each figurine, then knelt and rocked softly to and fro.

"Are you sick?" the merchant said as she stared down at Loi.

Loi quickly wiped her eyes and stood back up.

"Where did you get this carving, please?"

"Why, a young man brought it in just this morning. He had a whole sackful of them."

"Did he say where he was going or where he was living?"

"He was living on the streets, from the looks of him. All covered with dust and dirt, he was, especially his bare feet. I'd say he just came from a farming village. But a very talented artist. I told him I couldn't buy all his carvings today, but that I really need some statues of Buddha. He wasn't too happy about that, said he preferred to carve animals. But he said he would carve some Buddhas, if he could find the wood for it. Too bad animals don't sell that well around here."

"But he didn't tell you where he was going after here, or when he was coming back? Did he tell you his name?"

"No. Is he your brother or something?"

"Yes, something like that. See"—she reached inside her food sack and took out the water buffalo. "He carved this for me when we lived in the same village. We were engaged to be married, but . . . well, never mind. If you see him again, please tell him Loi is waiting for him at Amerasian Park. It's across from the Foreign Office."

"Hmmm. I don't know if he's coming back. He didn't sound like he was very interested in carving Buddhas. But if I see him, I'll give him your message." The woman's kind eyes studied Loi's disappointment a moment, then she put her hand on Loi's shoulder. "If you want to sell that carving of yours, I think I can buy one more."

Loi's fingers closed around the buffalo and felt the warmth of the wood. She remembered Khai's sweet face the morning he had given it to her and how he had called her his fairy from Mount Nam Nhuc. Then she remembered Joe's beaten face and the *cyclo* driver Hung. Gently she handed the buffalo to the woman.

"All right. I guess some things are more important than possessions, anyway," she whispered as the woman left to get a cigar box of money. When the woman counted it out, Loi saw that it was not quite enough to repay Hung. But it was more than she had thought the merchant would pay.

"Here. I can see that this little buffalo means a lot to you, so I'm going to set it on my table in the back of the room. It will be the last one I sell. That will give you more time, in case you want to return some day and buy it back." She smiled as she pressed the money into Loi's hand.

"Thank you, madam. You're one of the kindest people I've met in this city."

The lady clucked her tongue as she guided Loi toward the door.

"Well—you do remind me of someone I used to know. She would be about your age now." Her eyes misted over and she had a faraway look on her face. "Don't dawdle, now. If I see your young man, I'll give him the message. Check back with me tomorrow."

By the time Loi left the shop, the Soviets were far down the street, still looking and not buying. She limped as fast as she could to the fountain and waited for Hung and his *cyclo*. While sitting on the ledge, her mind whirled with questions. Could they really be Khai's carvings she had seen in the window? Without initials they could have been made by any young artist. If it was Khai, how would he ever find her?

When the sun was straight overhead, Loi heard the familiar squeaking brakes of a *cyclo* and looked up into Hung's grinning face.

"Hey, country girl, what a surprise. I didn't think I would ever see you again." He pushed his cap back and wiped his brow, then parked his *cyclo* and sat beside her.

"Why do you say that?" Loi asked curtly. "I told you I would repay you as soon as I earned some money." She fished the bills from her cloth sack and handed them to Hung. "I'm sorry it's not quite enough yet, but I will get the rest as soon as possible. Joe will help me when he gets better."

"Well, at least the streets were safe from him for a couple of days. The businesses around here ought to thank me for that." Hung chuckled, then as he looked down, he stopped laughing. "Your foot!"

Loi glanced at her throbbing foot. She hadn't noticed anything strange that morning, but now her foot was large and puffy.

"It will be all right. I just need to stay off it for a while." But even as she spoke, Loi felt a wave of nausea and a sudden flash of heat that made beads of sweat pop out on her forehead.

"Hung, I have to go now. Thank you again for helping Joe."

"Hey, wait, Loi. Maybe it's none of my business, but just how did you get this money? I wouldn't want to take it if it caused you to . . . well . . . to get into trouble."

"Don't worry. I got it by selling something very precious to me."

"That's what I was afraid of," Hung said with a heavy sigh, then glanced away. After a long pause, he looked back up. "Loi . . . a friend of mine, another *cyclo* driver, said he saw you on White Tiger Street near the opium den. I called him a liar to his face. I hope I wasn't wrong."

Another wave of heat flushed over Loi's face and a sharp lump blocked her voice. She wanted to speak, to deny his accusation, but it was so very near the truth that her heart ached with shame. She hung her head and stared at her arm and the three red scratches made by the umbrella girl's sharp nails.

Hung expelled air from his lungs. "I can see by the look on your face that my friend wasn't lying. Such a pity. I was going to ask you to stay with me and my sister until you leave for America. She needs help with her sewing business. But now . . . if she ever found out you were a White Tiger Street girl . . ."

"I didn't sell myself!" Loi screeched in a tiny, dry voice. "I did go there, but I couldn't go through with it. I got the money by selling a teakwood carving that a friend in my village gave me."

"A wood carving? Then why didn't you sell the carving first? Why even go to White Tiger Street?"

"Because the little figurine was very special to me."

"Hmmm . . . that wasn't a very wise choice, country girl. Decent girls don't even think about going to White Tiger Street. They go blocks out of the way to avoid being seen near it. You weren't very smart."

Loi sighed, then looked up into his face. "Does this mean your kind offer to stay at your house is being taken back?"

Hung shrugged, then balanced himself on the bicycle seat as he prepared to push off. "My sister is very strict. And the friend who saw you visits a lot. I wish you'd come to me before you acted so rashly. I'm sorry, Loi."

"I'm sorry, too, Hung. You've been so kind to me. You're about the only friend I've got, besides Joe. And I promise I'll pay you the rest of the money I owe as soon as Joe gets well enough to help out." Loi put her hand on the handlebars, but Hung pushed the *cyclo* off.

Hung jerked his cap down low and gave her a sideways glance as he pedaled out into the river of bicycles.

"Forget the money you owe me, country girl," he called over his shoulder. "From the looks of your foot, you'll be needing more medicine very soon."

"Hung! Don't be mad!" Loi shouted, but he ignored her and was soon swallowed up in the crowd.

Loi started to walk, but her first step sent a sharp jolt of pain up her leg. She looked down at the swollen, discolored foot. With a whimper of anguish and pain, she limped across the street and headed for Amerasian Park.

13

THE AMERICAN

THE LITTLE park Loi now called home had never seemed so far away to her as she limped painfully along. As she passed a Buddhist temple, two young monks with shaved heads, wearing billowy saffron robes, exited carrying baskets of fruit. Loi paused at the entrance. She didn't even have any money to put into the box to pay for a joss stick, but she knew she would be forgiven, so she wiped off her feet and entered the dark, cool room. She worked her way through the dragon-entwined pillars toward the golden statue of Buddha surrounded by colorful flowers and fresh fruit. The only other person in the room was a very old monk who chanted over and over, his fluid singsong voice broken only by the sequenced pounding of his hollow metal prayer wheel. Loi lit her incense, knelt, and prayed.

As she rested, she examined the carved dragon and phoenix embellishing the portals leading to a separate room. Hundreds of photos of deceased ancestors covered every inch of the altar. The photo of one old white-bearded man looked like the photo of her own great-grandfather, and Loi remembered that next week was the anniversary of his death. Her mother would be busy preparing his favorite foods, cleaning the altar, and inviting friends over to honor his memory. As Loi rose, pain shot through her foot and leg, making her grab the nearest pillar.

"Are you all right, little sister?" one of the young monks asked.

"Yes, brother. Thank you for your concern."

Though the orange robe hid the man's body, his arms were strong like a farmer's. He held her arm until she reached the front entrance.

"Wait here a moment," he said and left on silent feet, his long robe seeming to float over the polished marble floor. When he returned, he was carrying another basket of fruit. The sweet, ripe smell saturated the air.

"Please take something," he said softly.

"No, I couldn't. . . ."

"Please. There is more here than we can eat. We have to give away what we don't need." He smiled and pushed the basket closer.

Loi's eyes pored over the basket of delectable mangoes, bananas, oranges, and persimmons. She selected a large mango, then bowed and thanked him.

Loi limped outside and began the walk back to Amerasian Park. As she passed by the back of the temple, she noticed the other young monk distributing a similar basket of ripe fruit to a horde of beggars and children. Loi felt ashamed. Even Joe had not taken food from the temple, and she vowed she wouldn't tell him where the mango came from.

Finally arriving at the plum tree, she saw that Joe was gone. So were most of the other people in the park, too. Then she noticed that the line outside the Foreign Office looked unusual. A crowd had gathered in the street, blocking traffic. At first she thought there had been an accident, but she dismissed that idea because the crowd was too thick for someone to be lying in the street. As she came closer, the crowd buzzed like a fat fly caught in a spider's web. Since she was taller than most of the people, she could see over the tops of heads. One head, however, stood out above all the rest. The hat resting on top of it was a clean, powder blue bush hat, and the curls peeking from under the brim were red.

"Raymond Smith!" she whispered and began pressing through the bodies. But after about ten feet she could go no farther. The crowd was as impassable as a bamboo grove. Then she saw a shock of orange hair a few feet away.

"Joe! What's going on?"

Joe dropped to his knees and crawled between legs until he was beside Loi. Then he stood up.

"It's Americans! I can't believe it, real Americans! I've never seen anybody so tall!" Joe's awe-filled voice squeaked as he tried to see around the girl in front of him.

"Loi, hold me up so I can see better."

Loi was glad to see he had gotten over his fever and the swelling had gone down around his eyes. As she hoisted Joe up on her shoulders, the mango she was carrying fell to the street. A hand grabbed it and quickly vanished back into the crowd.

"*American, gimme five!*" Joe shouted at the top of his lungs in English and waved. As he bounced up and down, pain shot into Loi's foot. The American returned Joe's waves and smiled, then continued talking to those immediately around him, who pushed and chattered like a mob of hungry rats over a piece of meat.

"How can I get him to come over here?" Joe asked impatiently.

"His name is Raymond Smith," Loi said. "I met him in Da Lat."

Joe looked down into her face from an upside-down position, then grinned and waved again.

"*Raymond Smith, gimme five!*" he shouted over and over in English.

The tall American jerked his head up and looked at Joe. Then he stepped into the crowd, which parted like a school of fish. When he got close, Loi noticed that the American with the camera and hairy face was also there. The camera whined softly as he pointed it at the crowd. Occasionally he snapped a photo with a smaller camera, too, and handed out pictures to giggling children.

"*Hey, Raymond Smith, gimme five,*" Joe repeated in a voice hoarse from yelling. Joe held out his hand and Smith shook it, then lifted Joe down from Loi's shoulders.

"*Hello, Raymond Smith,*" Loi said, hoping she was pronouncing the American words correctly. She smiled and extended her hand, imitating Joe. The familiar government guide frowned when he saw her, but he diligently translated their conversation, while the curious crowd watched in silence.

"Aren't you the girl from Da Lat?" Smith asked, as he cocked his head sideways. "Loi, wasn't it?"

Loi blushed and nodded. "I'm honored that you remember me."

"Of course I do. No one else gave me a water buffalo carving. And I remember the division number of your American father because it was the same as mine. I'm glad you made it to Saigon. Have you registered in the Amerasian Homecoming Program yet?"

Loi nodded. "I registered, but I haven't gotten final approval and a visa yet. It takes a long time. Maybe months."

"Even years," Joe piped in.

"That's too bad. Where's your boyfriend? The one who carved the water buffalo?"

Loi felt her face turn red. "We got separated," she finally said. "But I'm waiting for him to join me so we can get married."

"And are you staying in that park across the street?"

"Yes."

"Oh, Loi, look at you. You've lost so much weight I hardly recognized you. What happened to your foot?"

"I stepped on some glass."

"Let me look at it."

They walked to the curb, where she sat down and unwrapped the bloodstained cloth as far as it would go. Smith grimaced and Loi herself saw for the first time that it was filled with a yellow discharge. The excitement had made her forget about the pain for a few moments, but now the throbbing returned stronger than before.

"Let's get you to a doctor. And your friend here looks like he could use a little medicine, too. What happened to him?"

Loi blushed when she heard the words translated for her. She didn't dare tell Raymond Smith about Joe's scheme to sell her body to a strange man and steal his money.

"Tell Mr. Smith that my friend was jumped in an alley by some bad teenage boys."

Smith shook his head when he heard the guide's interpretation. He turned and spoke rapidly to the man holding the cameras.

"We're going to take you and Joe to a doctor and get those cuts fixed up."

Loi didn't protest, not just because of the fever that was beginning to consume her body and the pain traveling up her leg, but because she wanted Joe to receive a doctor's examination, too.

Loi and Joe slid into the backseat of the government car, trying to keep from giggling. Joe ran his hands over the smooth leather upholstery and put his nose against the backseat and inhaled deeply. Then he rolled the window up and down, again and again, and stuck his head out and waved to everyone in the street.

"I'm going to America! I'm going to America!" he called out, and Loi was glad the guide decided not to translate.

The hospital office was filled with adults—some as pale as death, some spitting blood into spittoons—crying babies, and sick children. Loi felt her foot did not warrant going to a doctor. She wanted to tell Smith that she had received worse cuts before and lived through it, but she was afraid of offending the American, who paced the lobby like an angry tiger. They waited and waited, until his face grew red and he spoke in rapid, harsh words to the guide. Finally a nurse in a white uniform took Joe and Loi inside, gave them horrible shots with long needles, cleaned their wounds, and wrapped Loi's foot in white gauze. When the nurse wasn't looking, Loi retrieved the bloodstained piece of blue silk *ao dai* from the trash can. It had too many memories for her to part with it now.

Outside, the American leaned over and spoke directly into Joe's face, even though Joe couldn't understand.

"Are you hungry, Joe? Want to eat?" He made motions with his hands as if he were eating a bowl of rice. Joe's eyes lit up and he grabbed the American's hand.

"Follow Joe. I know where the best food in Saigon is."

But the guide snorted and refused to translate for Joe.

"The American will eat where he wants, *bui-doi*," the guide snapped.

Joe glanced at Loi, and when the guide turned his back, Joe stuck out his tongue and made a terrible face. Loi giggled and nodded in agreement.

"I wonder what he is really telling Raymond Smith about us," Joe whispered into her ear as they fell in step behind the tall man, whose long gait equaled about three of Loi's steps.

Back in the car, Loi and Joe watched the town roll by, turning from slums to the tall, majestic French buildings and expensive hotels. They wondered where they would eat, but it didn't matter. Anything would be better than dry French rolls. They were surprised when the car stopped in front of a clothing store.

"What's going on?" Joe sat up.

"The American wants to buy you some decent clothes. He's embarrassed to be seen with you inside the restaurant," the guide said curtly.

"I don't believe a word he says," Loi whispered. "I think Raymond Smith is just being kind to us." Joe nodded and tapped Smith on the shoulder.

"*Thank you very much, Raymond Smith*," he said in his most precise English.

"You're welcome," the tall man replied, then he laughed.

Inside the shop, Loi couldn't believe her good fortune. She didn't want to do anything to cause trouble, so she chose pants and a matching top with tiny pink flowers. Joe, however, felt no need for modesty and went straight for the most American-looking garments he could find, blue jeans and a T-shirt with a picture of Bruce Springsteen on the front, dark glasses, and a baseball cap. Then he went for the most expensive bottle of anti-lice shampoo on the shelf.

"Joe, don't be so greedy. It's not polite to take advantage of Raymond Smith." She made him put back the big bottle and take a very small size. "Just let him decide what to buy. Maybe he doesn't have enough money to buy all these things."

"Don't be stupid, country girl. All Americans are rich, I told you. Look at his smile. He loves us to be happy. Don't spoil his fun. Here, take these shoes. Real shoes with hard soles, so you won't step on any more glass."

Loi reluctantly took the shoes, but when Joe wasn't looking she put them back and selected a pair of simple pink plastic thongs. They changed into the fresh clothes and rode to Maxim's Restaurant on Dong Khoi Street.

Loi had hoped that Joe would settle down once inside the restaurant, but he was wilder than ever, ordering everything he had ever heard of, touching the crisp white linen tablecloth, smelling the fresh lily in the single vase, and going to the rest room three times. The last time he came out, his orange hair was wet and smelling of pungent shampoo and slicked straight back with a comb he had stolen from the store when Raymond Smith wasn't looking. The guide gave Joe scorching glares and refused to translate any of his requests, but there was plenty of food anyway.

Loi took small, delicate bites, but Joe pigged everything down and slopped food all over his face. Several times when she glanced across the table, she saw Smith staring at her and she noticed that he ate very little. Afterwards, while the men drank beers and Loi had a sweet bean-gelatin-coconut milk drink, Joe and the cameraman exchanged words, each trying to teach the other how to say "Look at that good-looking babe" in his own language.

"Raymond Smith," Loi said softly, hoping the guide would translate correctly. "Have you located your own Amerasian daughter yet?"

From the painful expression that swept over Smith's face and the long sigh that escaped his lips, she knew the answer.

"No, Loi, I haven't. The Amerasian Park was my last hope. She wasn't there, but I did find out that her mother died about four years ago. My daughter went to live with a relative, but no one knows where or the name. It's almost hopeless now."

"I'm very sorry for you. And for her. If I had an American father like you, I would be the happiest girl in the world. I will pray for her and for you tonight."

Raymond Smith smiled, then he rolled the linen napkin up and tucked it under the china plate decorated with blue dragons.

"Loi, I've been thinking all the time I have been here in Vietnam. I know I will probably never find my own child, but I want to help in some way. Help repay the women of Vietnam who were left behind with babies to raise. I know now how difficult life has been for all of them."

Loi said nothing but listened to the man's strange words, so full of emotion, and watched the pale blue eyes glisten. When the guide spoke, the words were without feeling.

"I have decided that I would like to take an Amerasian child back to America with me. I've already made arrangements with the government for one person and completed all the paperwork. I had hoped it would be my daughter, but . . . Loi, I would like to take you in her place and sponsor you. I can see you're intelligent and determined. With a good education, you can be anything you want in America. And we might even be able to locate your father. There are organizations that help Amerasians find their fathers. I can read his division number on his sleeve in that photo you have. He was in the same division as me—a couple of years later, though. I can do some checking with the army for you."

Loi felt the blood drain from her face. She swallowed and looked into the guide's cold eyes. It was definitely hatred she saw there.

"Did I understand Raymond Smith?" she asked. "He wants me to go to America with him instead of his daughter?"

The guide repeated the question, then confirmed the reply.

Joe jerked to attention in his seat and dropped the chopsticks from his grease-covered hands.

"Hey, wait. You're going to America, country girl? Already?" He faced the guide. "Ask Raymond Smith to take Joe, too. I'm a good boy. Very smart. I could become very rich."

The guide shook his head. "Forget it. He doesn't

want trash like you. You'd be better off in jail. Better off for the streets of Ho Chi Minh City."

"No, no! You tell him what I said!" Joe stood on his chair. "Raymond Smith, take me, too! Tell him I have to go. I'll die if I have to stay here one more day."

Tears streamed from Joe's eyes as he slumped back into the chair and pounded his fists on the table.

"Little brother, don't worry," Loi whispered as she put her arm around his shaking shoulders. "I won't go with him. I'll stay here with you."

Joe's tears stopped abruptly, and he jerked his head up.

"No, sister, you have to go. When you get to America, you save up money and send for me as a sponsor. I know that's the only way I will ever get to America. Nobody else there wants me. Nobody wants me here, either."

Smith watched the scene, then reached over and clasped Joe's hand.

"I'm sorry I can't take you, Joe. I only have a visa and papers approved for one person. But we can send for you later. We won't forget you. I promise."

Joe sniffed, wiped his runny nose on his new T-shirt, then smiled. "Okay, Raymond Smith. I'll wait for you."

Smith grinned. "Gimme five!" He shoved his hand out and Joe took it. Then Smith turned back to Loi.

"So, it's settled? You're coming back with me?"

Loi stared at the plate of food scraps and bit her lip. Joe jabbed her in the ribs.

"What's the matter with you, country girl? You should be dancing for happiness. Isn't this what you wanted?"

"Yes, but . . ."

"Is something wrong?" Smith asked the guide when Loi didn't give an answer right away. The guide shrugged, and Joe stared at her in disbelief.

"Big sister, what's wrong?"

"It's just that I promised Khai I would wait for him."

After hearing the translation, Smith leaned back in his chair.

"Ahhh . . . I see. You don't want to leave him behind?"

Loi met his eyes and nodded. "I know he's looking for me."

"I understand your dilemma. It's very hard to leave someone you love behind and go to another country. I made that same decision myself twenty years ago and have never been the same since. If you decide not to go, I'll understand. But I'm leaving tomorrow. If you want to come with me, meet me at the Foreign Office at eight o'clock A.M. My plane leaves at four o'clock and we have to get papers filled out at Tan Son Nhut Airport before you can leave. And you must have a medical exam. If you're not

213

there, I will know you decided to stay in Vietnam and wait for your friend, Khai. The choice is yours. No matter what you decide, I wish you the best of luck." He reached into his pocket and took out some bills. "Please take this in case you need to buy something for the trip." He lifted her hand to his lips and placed a soft kiss there.

After the Americans left and Loi and Joe were walking back to the park, Joe punched her ribs again.

"Are you crazy? Nobody turns down the chance to go to America. Especially with a rich, nice man like Raymond Smith to sponsor you like a father. Forget about that buffalo boy. He'll never come after you, anyway." Joe angrily jerked up a weed growing through a crack in the sidewalk.

"Oh, but I'm sure he's in Saigon looking for me. I saw some of his carvings over on Hoa Binh Street. Help me find him, Joe. If he marries me, he can come to America, too."

At first, Joe refused to help her, but when he saw how determined she was, he gave in. First they checked back at the shop on Hoa Binh Street. The shop owner had sold one of the carvings but had not seen Khai again. Loi left another message, this time explaining that she must find Khai before eight o'clock tomorrow morning.

Joe knew the neighborhood well and pointed out the shops that were most likely to buy wood carvings of water buffaloes. But the trail began and ended on that street, for no one knew where the tall, quiet farm boy had vanished to, and no one knew his name. In her heart, Loi knew it was Khai, but a part of her brain told her she had no real proof. A lot of men carved animals to sell. And most of them looked like they had come from a farm village.

The day passed and Loi's foot ached, but she could not stop the search. By curfew time, she was no closer to finding Khai than she had been that morning and had to give it up.

When Loi crawled onto the old straw mat, the word had already spread through the park that she was going to America, and she was the envy of everyone. Joe fell asleep quickly, looking strange lying there in his new clothes, the red baseball cap tugged low over his eyes. But Loi could not sleep. She listened to the distant groan and creak of the bamboo that sounded like ghosts playing eerie flutes, accompanied by yelping dogs down the street. Someone was brewing jasmine tea, and its sweet fragrance drifted on the soft wind. Lanterns cast dancing shadows on the office across the street until, one by one, they went out. But still Loi did not sleep.

She removed the photograph from her pocket and tilted it until the light of the waning moon shed its pale glow on the glossy paper. She had not looked at it since last Thursday. That was the day when Mrs. Dung and her friend, who both came from Da Nang, had peered over Loi's shoulder at the photo. The women laughed and whispered as they pointed at the couple standing in front of a tall stucco building.

"Did you know my mother?" Loi had asked anxiously. But Mrs. Dung's friend turned her head aside and spat.

"No, but I knew that building. Most of the women who lived there were unwed mothers or prostitutes who sold their bodies for a meal. I would never have allowed myself to be photographed in front of it, even if I didn't live there." Then everyone else had laughed, too.

A single tear slid down Loi's cheek as she looked at the smiling American soldier and her mother's sweet, calm face. Was that the house that she remembered in her dream? Had her mother been just another working girl like the umbrella girl of White Tiger Street? Was that why her mother refused to tell her anything about her father—his name, where he came from, how they met? Was it because her mother had not even known which man was the father of her child? Was the blue-eyed soldier in the photograph just one of a hundred customers?

Loi returned the photo to the pocket of her new pants, then rolled onto her side and closed her eyes. She listened to the wind rattling through the plum tree, but she did not sleep.

14

THE DECISION

LOI WAS dreaming about the American soldier again. She was sitting on the same sticky floor, wearing the same red dress. But this time when the tall man with the twinkling blue eyes picked her up, he carried her out the door. And even though Loi was in his arms, going down the stairs, she could see her mother standing at the door crying. Then she saw Khai running after them as they boarded a plane.

With a start, Loi sat up and listened. She heard the sad, hollow wail of the bamboo rubbing together. It was, in a way, a strangely beautiful sound because it reminded her of the haunting melodies Khai often played on his bamboo flute while he tended the water buffaloes. Suddenly she wished she still had the teakwood carving to hold, and she missed Khai more than ever.

It was so early that even the old man with the white goatee had not yet started his morning *tai chi*. Joe was still sleeping soundly. Sometime during the night his baseball cap had come off and now lay a short distance away. As Loi replaced it on his head, she could smell the pungent fragrance of medicinal shampoo radiating from his orange hair.

Loi sneaked out of the park and quietly walked toward the merchant shop where she had sold the teak carving. She would check one final time for messages from Khai. The swelling in her foot had gone down, and it only hurt when she put her full weight on it. By tiptoeing she could almost walk without a limp. As she passed a small cemetery, she rapidly crossed the street. There was no point in tempting the ghosts that might still be wandering about.

Loi heard a sudden screech, and a flurry of gray fur dashed across her feet toward a gutter. Seconds later a gray cat emerged again, its jaws locked around a squirming rat. Loi shivered and crossed her arms. Seeing a cat in the morning was a sign of bad luck for the rest of the day. And since she had been born in the Year of the Rat, the luck would be doubly bad.

On Hoa Binh Street the merchant shops had not yet opened, so Loi sat on the curb to watch dawn streak across the sky over the tops of buildings like fingers of pink silk. Old women stepped outside their doors, and with short-handled brooms they swept the walks and yards free of dirt and piles of red betel-leaf juice. Roosters began to stretch their necks and crow, while chickens pecked at the ground for crumbs and insects.

Eventually Loi heard clinking utensils and smelled the aroma of steeping tea and fresh rice coming from under the door of the shop behind her. She stood and pressed her face against the dirty display window. The buffalo with the white streak was still there, its sad face staring back at her with a placid expression. Loi touched the pocket of her new pants and felt the bulge of money Raymond Smith had given her. If she had only had that money yesterday, she wouldn't have sold her precious carving. Loi hoped the merchant would keep her promise and sell it back to her. Maybe it was foolish of her to waste the money on a mere wood carving, but if she was going to America, it would be the only reminder she would have of Khai.

When the shop doors finally opened, the owner's wife immediately noticed Loi and invited her inside. After hearing that Loi was going to America, the woman smiled and took the teak carving from her table.

"Here, you can take it back for free. I have a sister-in-law in Portland, Oregon. Let me give you a letter to mail to her." The woman scurried behind a faded red curtain and soon a man's excited voice joined in. In a few minutes, the lady returned from behind the curtain, smiling and carrying a cup of steaming tea.

"Please sit and drink tea with me. We will celebrate your going to America. My husband and I have lots of family there."

Loi bowed in thanks and sipped the hot tea. It was of far better quality than the tea Mrs. Dung shared, and it reminded Loi of the tea she had tasted at Huong's wedding over a year ago. She and Khai had mingled into the crowd, slipping up to each other and lightly touching fingertips when no one was looking. They had exchanged secret smiles and glances, and although Khai had said nothing, Loi had known he was thinking of their own wedding.

Loi finished the tea just as a balding man entered the room, holding a folded sheet of paper. His wife read it quickly, then folded it again and pressed it into Loi's hand.

"We don't have an envelope or stamp for it. If you could please mail it for us when you get to the United States, we would be so grateful. Her address is written here on the outside." The woman hugged Loi, and the man bowed and wished her luck.

"Don't read it, please," the man said. "It is very personal." Loi nodded and promised. She didn't want to tell them that she could only read printed words and would not understand his handwriting.

"Has the farm boy who carved the buffaloes returned yet? Did he get my message?"

The woman shook her head sadly. "Sorry, he has not returned."

Loi sighed and tried to swallow down the hard lump that blocked her speech. "Please ask him if his name is Khai. If it is, tell him Loi has gone to America. Tell him . . . I waited . . . I tried to find him." Her voice broke as she imagined the shocked and pained expression on Khai's face, the grief of betrayal in his heart. With all her strength she forced the rest of the sentence out. "Tell him if he wants to marry another girl, I will understand. Tell him I love him."

Loi darted from the shop into the bright morning sunlight. Already bicycles and *cyclos* swished by and cafés overflowed with men sipping coffee. Old men hung bamboo cages beside their chairs and listened to the merry chirping finches while they ate bowls of *pho* or read newspapers.

Loi paused for a brightly colored funeral wagon moving slowly down the street. A large photograph of the deceased person hung from the front and a line of mourners draped in loose white cloth and wearing white headbands followed. A skinny old man whose spindly legs didn't look strong enough to lift themselves slammed two brass cymbals together while a younger man beat a drum. As the short procession passed by, Loi caught the fragrance of flowers and incense.

"Good," she whispered to herself and smiled. Seeing a funeral early in the morning was an omen of good luck to come. Perhaps it would cancel out the bad luck of the gray cat.

By the time Loi returned to Amerasian Park, the air was warm and she itched all over from her new clothes. When Joe saw her approach, he ran to meet her.

"Where have you been? I was worried that somebody had kidnapped you. You look like a rich girl now in those clothes."

Loi was glad to see that Joe was feeling up to his old mischievous self, even though his face still looked chopped up.

"I went to the merchant shop to buy back Khai's water buffalo," she explained and removed the carving from the red plastic purse that Raymond Smith had insisted she buy.

"You spent your money on that?"

"No, the owner gave it back. But that reminds me. Here, I want you to have the money. I won't need it in America with Raymond Smith." She removed the money from her pocket and handed it to Joe.

Joe's eyes widened, then they grew soft and sad.

"I've got ten thousand, thousand things to tell you about America," he said firmly, and he led her to a park bench occupied by a flock of goldfinches.

"First, after you settle down, write me and give me your address."

"Joe, you don't know how to read and write, do you?"

"No problem. My friend Bob can do that for me. Then you find somebody coming over here and ask them to bring me some things. I need a *stereo*—the kind with batteries—tapes of *Bruce Springsteen* and *Madonna*, and a color TV, more *blue jeans*, and *polo shirts*. You know what size I am. Don't worry about me growing any bigger."

"But I'm not rich. How can I buy all those things? One TV costs more than three years' wages."

"You can do it. Everybody in America is rich. I promise you—you can buy anything you want over there."

"Joe . . . I can't promise . . . How can I send you a letter? You don't even have an address."

"Just say, Amerasian Park across from the Foreign Office on Bui Thi Xuan Street. Everybody here knows Joe. Please. I would do the same for you, big sister."

"All right. I promise."

"And for me, go to a *baseball* game one time and eat one *hotdog* and one *popcorn* and *peanuts*."

"What is *popcorn*?"

"I don't know. But you have to do it and say, 'I am eating this for my little brother, Joe, so I won't forget him.' " Joe reached into the back pocket of his new blue jeans. "I almost forgot to show you this. Bill, the cameraman, took this. I give it to you so you won't forget me."

"I won't forget you, Joe," Loi said softly as she took the photo. The orange hair was combed back and the freckles had been washed off, so he almost looked handsome.

"Sure, of course not. You're not like the others who left. They were all cheap-hearts. They didn't really like me. Even Quan. He promised every-thing." Joe exhaled a long sigh. He stared across the park deep in thought for a moment, and Loi wondered how many times Joe had gotten close to girls or boys scheduled for America. How many times had he gone over his list of dreams and asked someone to eat *popcorn* in his name? Had every single one of them simply forgotten Joe and Amerasian Park?

"I won't forget you," Loi repeated as she put her arm around his thin shoulders. He looked up at her and smiled, then wrapped his skinny arms around her waist and leaned his head on her arm. She could smell the scent of fresh shampoo and knew he'd washed his hair again.

Suddenly Joe sat up and twisted his head around. "I think I hear people talking about Raymond Smith. Let's go."

"But it's not time yet."

"Maybe he's come early."

A sick feeling crept through Loi's stomach, and she wasn't sure she would be able to keep from vomiting.

"I don't feel too good," she whispered and wiped beads of sweat from her forehead. Joe leaned closer and examined her face.

"You're whiter than a plum blossom. But I know what it is. You ate too much last night. Me, too. I got a little sick early this morning, but it goes away fast. Lie down on the bench a few minutes. I'll go check to see if it is Raymond Smith."

Loi decided not to tell Joe that she was sick with fear at the thought of going to America. He would never understand. She stretched out on the wooden slats of the bench and put the red purse under her head for a pillow. Soon her head stopped spinning and her stomach calmed down, but the shaking would not go away. The thunder of her heart drowned out the sounds around her.

Loi saw some people moving about, forming a crowd at the end of the park near the Foreign Office. Occupants of the park began walking faster, women grabbing the hands of their Amerasian sons and daughters and small grandchildren. Soon the chattering sounded like a flock of ravens in a banyan tree. Loi didn't have to look; she knew Raymond Smith had come early.

"What am I doing? What am I doing?" she whispered out loud, then sat up. "How can I go without

Khai?'' Loi's brain reeled as she thought about Khai running after the bus and his earnest plea for her to wait for him. If she went on to America, she would never see Khai again. Surely there was not another boy as good and kind and loving as Khai. But what if he didn't come to Saigon looking for her? What if his parents had forced him to marry Suong, or some terrible accident had befallen him? There was no guarantee that the wood carvings were his. And if she gave up this chance of going to America with Raymond Smith, when would she ever have another opportunity to find her American father? Raymond Smith had promised to help her find the soldier in the photo. Without his aid, how could she ever find the truth of why he left her behind? And if she didn't seize this opportunity, how much longer would she have to wait for her name to appear on the list? Some people had been waiting for years. And Loi was not sure she could last even another day on the streets of Saigon.

Suddenly Loi's stomach lurched, and she vomited onto the grass. When she looked up she saw Joe running toward her, followed by a group of hysterical women and teenagers.

"Loi, hurry!" Joe shouted. "Raymond Smith is ready to leave. He's asking for you."

Loi stood and glanced around the park one final time. At least she would not miss this miserable place with its sad faces and sickness and desperation. Almost any place would be better than here.

But before Loi could take Joe's hand, the mob reached the bench and surrounded her. Women shouted names and addresses and shoved scraps of paper with messages on them into her pockets. One woman wailed and pulled her own hair and fainted, only to be stepped on by a hundred feet. Loi tried to take the messages, but soon her red purse overflowed, and the hands frantically stuffing notes into her pockets accidentally ripped her new blouse. Some of the women had no names to give her, but simply wanted to touch her for good luck. But not all of the touches were kind, and Loi felt a sharp pain in her back.

"Come on," Joe shouted above the shrieks as he grabbed Loi's hand. Slowly they plowed through the mob toward the waiting Americans, who were busy fighting off their own riot. Loi pressed her hands over her ears and stepped behind Raymond Smith, but even there, hands found her.

"Loi! Take this message to my sister!"

"Loi! Over here! Give this to my cousin!"

"Loi! Wait for me!"

Loi wanted to scream as she and the Americans slowly backed up onto the steps of the Foreign Office. She tried to find Joe's orange hair but saw only desperate, sad faces and hundreds of hands waving pieces of paper and hats to get her attention. Someone was waving a red-and-yellow scarf that reminded her of the one Officer Hiep had given her. Suddenly Loi thought about her cousins, her mother, and her Uncle Long. She would never see them again. Never be able to explain that she was really alive and still loved them. Nor would she ever see the green rice fields undulating in the wind or the rugged mountains shrouded in blue mists. No more monkeys and parrots chattering in the jungles or water buffaloes sunk up to their noses in muddy pools. No more Vietnam. Tears slid down her cheeks and blurred the faces below into a haze.

Raymond Smith took Loi's arm, inhaled deeply, then pushed through the crowd toward the small white van with the words "Saigon Tourism" printed on the side.

"Loi, wait for me!" Someone shouted from the crowd.

Loi heard the words again and turned her head. The red-and-yellow scarf was closer, waving above the cone-shaped hat of the owner. Loi blinked, then rubbed her eyes until she brought the scarf into focus. Could it be?

"Khai!" she screamed with all her might, breaking free from Smith's hand and leaping into the crowd. She felt as if she were swimming through a river of bodies as she screamed again and again, keeping her eyes on the scarf. Suddenly it disappeared into the mob. Panic rushed over Loi as her eyes swept over the calling faces.

"Loi!" the voice shouted. She turned just as Khai stumbled from the crowd and bumped into her. They threw their arms around each other, and Loi buried her face against his damp neck.

"When did you arrive?"

"The morning it rained so hard."

"It was the one day I didn't check the bus station. So, the rain brought good luck after all."

"I got your message from the shop owner only a few minutes ago. I was afraid you'd be gone before I found you," Khai said.

"Forgive me for thinking of leaving you behind, Khai. But now that you're here, we can marry and both go to America."

"No. I can't, Loi. That's why I had to find you— to tell you that I can't live in America, or in a big city. I've wrestled with this ever since you left. I'll always love you, but my home is here in Vietnam, the land where my ancestors are buried."

Loi felt the blood drain from her face and her head went giddy. "But what about our plans?"

"Stay in Vietnam with me, Loi. Be the wife of a simple farmer and the mother of happy children."

"But your family, and my uncle? And your brother Quy? What about them? They won't let us marry."

"Everything has been taken care of. I finally worked up the courage to speak to your uncle and told him how I felt about you. He was very willing for us to marry. Compared to Officer Hiep, I'm a hero."

"But . . . how? I am supposed to be dead."

"I will explain all that in a minute. Then I spoke to my father. When he learned I was going to run away to Saigon or America just to be with you, he changed his mind. He said he would rather I stayed with him and help with the farming than go to a strange land. He said he would help me build a hut and get started. Quy was furious, but he doesn't dare speak out against our father."

Loi sighed. She was confused and couldn't think for all the noise and pushing of the crowd closing in on them. Finally, she shouted, "But what about my American father? Am I just to give him up forever? Could you give up your father, Khai?"

"I want you to stay, Loi, more than anything in the world. But if you have to go, I will understand." Khai's rough, warm hands closed around Loi's fingers. Then she felt a tug at her sleeve.

"Big sister, the Americans want to leave now," a quivering voice said, and she looked down into a pale, frightened little face covered with bruises and cuts and tears.

"Joe, this is Khai. I've finally found him."

"Hello, Khai. But, sister, the Americans are in

the bus waiting for you. Please hurry." Loi, Joe, and Khai pushed through the crowd to the Saigon Tourism van. Smith waved them inside.

"Come on, all of you can ride with us to the airport," he said as he helped each one climb inside.

After they had settled down, Khai opened a bag he carried over his shoulder and removed something. Loi recognized it immediately—a red wedding *ao dai* with large peonies carefully embroidered on its front panel. Khai gently laid it on Loi's lap.

"This is from your mother—a gift for our wedding."

"From Má? But . . . but surely she must think I'm dead."

Khai shook his head. "No, she saw through our scheme. She insisted on sewing this for you; that's why it took me so long to come to Saigon. She said she understands why you did it."

"But how did she get the money for this wedding *ao dai?*"

"Her vegetables sold well."

A sharp pain cracked Loi's heart and shame filled her soul. She quickly turned her head and watched the scenery flying by in a blur.

"Khai? Did my Uncle Long . . . what happened to him? Did Officer Hiep believe that I was killed in an accident? Or did he see through the scheme, too?"

Khai chuckled. "Oh, they didn't even have to tell him that story. Hiep sent a messenger to your uncle.

You see, his old mother gave him a terrible time because you were Amerasian and because you acted so
rudely at the engagement party. She fought with
Hiep constantly. She refused to take care of his five
children and claimed that he was disgracing the family name by marrying you. I guess he decided you
were not worth the burden of his mother's wrath."

"When did that happen?"

"The day after you ran away."

"Then if I had only waited one more day, everything would have worked itself out. If only I had been
more patient." Loi sighed and looked back out the
window. "I am so foolish."

"No, you're not, Loi. After all, you have an opportunity to go to America now, if you choose. I
think at least a million people would gladly trade
places with you right now."

"Make that a million and one," Joe said as he
turned his nose from the window. Loi reached across
the seat and squeezed his small, dirty hand.

"You will go to America someday, Joe. I promise."

Joe shrugged, then put his nose back to the glass.

As Loi looked at Joe's sad face, she felt a pain in
her heart. He wanted to go to America more than
anything—to wear American clothes, to eat American food, to breathe American air. It meant everything to him. And when Joe talked about California,
it sounded like paradise. His desperation to go should
make her feel all the luckier. She should be happy for

a kind, sincere man like Raymond Smith to take care of her, to send her to school, to help her find her father. Maybe her father had children. That would mean Loi had sisters or brothers. Maybe they would love and accept her and not call her *con-lai* and *bui-doi*. Her heart should be beating with excitement and joy. And yet . . .

Loi raised her eyes and looked at Khai's handsome face. A sudden lump rose to her throat, so sharp and painful that no amount of swallowing would force it down. She knew she would not be able to speak again, that if she only managed to say "good-bye," they would be the hardest words she had ever said in her life.

"Loi." Khai's soft voice broke into her thoughts. "I have something else from your mother. She wrote you a letter."

Loi took the faded, stained piece of paper, which she recognized as a sheet from one of her little cousins' school primers. With trembling fingers she unfolded the sheet and slowly began reading her mother's large, simple printing.

My dearest beloved daughter, I feel it is time you learned the truth about your American father . . .

15

THE HOMECOMING

"I SEE THE airport up ahead," Khai said as the tour van slowed for a turn. "I want you to know that I will understand if you choose to go to America instead of marrying me. It's a wonderful—"

"I'm not going," Loi interrupted.

"What?" Joe whirled around, his oily nose leaving a streak across the window. "Are you crazy? You *have* to go!"

Loi removed all the scraps of paper that desperate mothers had stuffed into her pockets and red purse.

"Khai, can I have that sack around your neck?"

He nodded and handed it to her. Loi placed all the notes into the sack, leaving her purse void of everything except Joe's picture, the teakwood buffalo, and the photograph of the American soldier. She studied the photo a long time, then flipped it over.

"Excuse me, do you have something to write with?" she asked the guide, who reluctantly handed her a fountain pen. Loi awkwardly copied the American name and address from her mother's letter on the back of the picture. She returned the pen, then handed the photo to Joe. Joe squinted his eyes and screwed up his face.

"What's this for?"

"You may need it to prove that you're half American."

"What!" Joe slid to the edge of his seat.

"I've decided to stay in Vietnam with Khai."

"Loi, no." Khai took the photo from Joe and pushed it back into Loi's hand. "If going to America and finding your father is what you really want, I cannot stand in your way."

But Loi refused the photo and shook her head. Then she turned to the guide again.

"Please tell Raymond Smith that I have decided to stay here and marry Khai. If Smith could take Joe to America in my place, I would be very grateful. The photo will prove that he is half American, in case he has some trouble at the airport."

Loi sat quietly as the guide interpreted her words. Smith scratched his head, glanced at the cameraman, then shrugged.

"Please tell Raymond Smith," she continued, "that someday I may come visit him in America, with Khai. But Joe will never, never have another chance like this to go. Please, Raymond Smith, let him go in my place. He will be a good boy."

Smith whispered to the cameraman a few minutes, then smiled. He shook Khai's hand, then Loi's while the guide translated.

"Mr. Smith says he will get Joe to America. He will write Joe's name on the papers instead of yours. He will arrange a medical exam and talk to the authorities. If necessary, he will claim to be Joe's father and pay more money." The guide frowned, as if he found the topic of bribery too distasteful to speak of. "Smith also extends his congratulations on getting married, Miss Loi and Mr. Khai. He says he knows it was a hard decision. He wishes you many long, happy, and healthy years."

Smith reached into his wallet and withdrew a small white card and an American hundred-dollar bill. "Smith says, here is a wedding present for you. And that card has his address and phone number on it. If you ever do come to America, call or write."

The van stopped in front of the Tan Son Nhut Airport and Smith slid open the van door, then turned to Joe.

"Well, Joe, are you ready to go to America?" the guide translated.

"I've been ready all my life," Joe said, then leapt across the seat and wrapped his arms and legs around Smith, while tears streamed down his cheeks. Smith laughed, and Bill, the cameraman, ruffled Joe's orange hair and sniffed.

While the men unloaded their luggage and said farewell to the guide, Joe threw his arms around Loi and pressed his tear-stained face to her stomach.

"Good-bye, sister. Don't worry. I will find this American father of yours and tell him you're a number-one good-looking daughter. I'll send you a tape player and lots of *Madonna* tapes. And *blue jeans* for the buffalo boy."

"And don't forget to eat one *popcorn* in my name and think of me," she teased as she tweaked his ugly nose.

Joe laughed, then dug out the roll of Vietnamese money.

"Here, I won't be able to use this in America," he said as he pushed it into Loi's hands.

In return, Loi handed him the little teak buffalo she had carried for so long.

"Don't forget Vietnam," she said softly. Joe waved, then he ran after the men. As they disappeared into the terminal building, Loi and Khai started walking down the road. They caught a pedicab back to town.

After waiting near the bus station for several hours for the next bus to Da Lat they heard the roar of an airplane rip through the sky. Loi looked up at the streak of silver with its tail of black smoke. She waved, in case it was Joe's plane, but couldn't see any faces.

"I'm hungry. Shall we eat?" Loi asked, pointing to a soup stand set up under a tall tamarind tree near the Saigon River.

While waiting for the owner to bring them bowls of *pho*, Loi laid out the red *ao dai* on the table and ran her hand over the cool silk.

"Are you ready to wear the wedding dress today?" Khai asked.

"No," Loi said slowly. "I think I would prefer to get married in our village. I want my family and yours to be there for the ceremony. And it should be on the day set by the astrologers. Everything must be perfect and respectful. We have enough money to buy bus tickets now. And this one hundred American dollars is a whole year's income. We can build our own little hut and furniture. We won't have to ask for anything from your family. We'll be just as well-off as any newlyweds."

"And I've learned that my teak carvings can be very profitable. Between planting seasons, I can carve more and sell them at Da Lat."

"And I am going to walk into that school and learn to read and write properly. I don't care what that mean-eyed teacher says. I have as much right as anyone." Loi squeezed Khai's hand as the owner brought out the steaming bowls of noodles covered with thin slices of undercooked beef. They ate hungrily, then returned to the bus station.

Even though they had money now, they bought the cheapest tickets and sat on top of the rusty old green DeSoto when it finally arrived. Soon they had left behind the sounds and stink of the city, and Loi breathed in the fresh, fragrant country air. After a few miles had rumbled by, Khai cleared his throat.

"Loi, you don't have to tell me what was in the letter . . . But aren't you even a little sorry that you gave up the chance to go to America and find your father? You did write his name and address on the back of the photo, didn't you?"

"He wasn't my father."

"What?"

"He was just a kind soldier who found my mother after she had given birth to me. He felt sorry for her and took us under his wing for a long time. But my mother didn't sleep with him; he already had a wife and children."

"Oh. But then, who was your real father?"

Loi turned her head and watched the empty rice paddies passing by. Already men and water buffaloes had plowed under the stubble and were softening the earth for the next planting. Women were hoisting baskets of water from irrigation ditches into the smaller flood paddies, where rice seeds would be sown to sprout into seedlings for transplanting. One of the boys sitting atop a buffalo cow waved at them and Loi waved back. Then she turned to Khai.

"Má didn't know my father's name. He was just a boy, lonely and scared like her. She slept with him once and never saw him again."

Khai swallowed hard, then glanced down at his large, rough hands.

"I'm sorry, Loi. I didn't mean to pry. That's a terrible thing to learn about your own mother."

"No. No, it isn't. She did what she had to. You see, her mother was dying and all her older brothers were in the army—some for the north, some for the south. She was the only daughter. They had nothing, no way to earn money. They had already sold everything they owned and lived in a little shack made of pieces of American scrap and trash."

"It must have been awful for her. I heard she had a nice home in Hue when she was a child."

"Yes, and she had dreamed of marrying a mandarin's son. When her mother got deathly sick, Má did the only thing she knew. She went into Da Nang to beg. An American soldier gave her money in exchange for sleeping with him. She never asked his name."

"But at least her mother got the medicine."

"Yes, the medicine cured my grandmother Nguyen, but when she found out Má was pregnant, she disowned her and kicked her out. By that time her oldest daughter-in-law had found a place for the family to live. But they wouldn't let Má come with them. I was born on the side of a street early in the morning hours. No one helped her. That's where the soldier in the photo found her."

"Wouldn't it have been easier for her to abandon you?"

"Like Joe's mother abandoned him," Loi whispered, then shivered. "Má was seventeen, the same as me. No one would marry her, because of me. I wonder what I would have done in her place?"

Khai pulled her close and wrapped his arms around her from behind.

"I doubt that you ever would have slept with a soldier for money. You would have thought of something else to do. Something right and honorable."

Loi swallowed hard and thought about the girls on White Tiger Street. It was only by miracle that she wasn't there with them.

"Maybe there can be no honor in times of war," Loi said softly. "That is why I have to return to our village and speak to my mother. I must let her know that it was a courageous thing she did. To tell her she should not be ashamed. And to thank her."

"Maybe it would be better to live in another village, Loi. Or near Da Lat. Some of the people in our village have given you much pain over the years."

But Loi stubbornly shook her head.

"No. Perhaps that has been my problem all along.

My mother and Uncle Long have taught me to always run and hide my face. To cram my curly hair up under my *non-la* and stare at the ground. I know they did it out of love, to protect me from cruel remarks. But no more." Loi swooped her pointed straw hat off her head and thrust her face into the wind. The air whistled in her ears as it pushed her soft curls back from her flushed cheeks. "I have finally learned that I am as much a part of this country as those villagers. Whether they like it or not, my umbilical cord is buried in the earth of Vietnam just like theirs."

"You are very brave," Khai said as he studied her dark, determined eyes. For a few minutes the only sound was the clank and moan of the green bus. Then Khai spoke again.

"Tell me truthfully. After being in Saigon and seeing so many modern things, didn't you want to go to America and become rich? Don't you feel at least a little regret?"

Loi turned and faced Khai.

"No. I wasn't going to America for riches. I was going to find my father—to ask him how he could leave me behind, his own flesh and blood. I wasn't sure whether I loved him or hated him, but I had to find the answer. But now, I know the answer." Loi drew in a deep breath and let it out slowly. Then she smiled. "Besides, I am already rich. And do you know what I want right now more than anything?"

Khai raised one eyebrow. "No," he said cautiously.

"I want to hear the song of the buffalo boy."

They laughed. Then Khai raised his voice and sang a sweet, haunting melody—the same love song that he had awakened her with every morning.

Loi leaned back against his chest and sighed. It was still the most beautiful sound on earth.

AUTHOR'S NOTE

Song of the Buffalo Boy is set in the year 1989. Since that time, a few changes have occurred in the Amerasian Homecoming Program. The program, created in 1987 to expedite the exit of sons and daughters of American soldiers, initially had the goal of bringing 27,000 Amerasians and their families to the United States by March 1990. However, the deadline was extended to the end of 1992, and the estimated number of eligible immigrants increased to 81,000.

Another important development was the creation of the Amerasian Transit Center in 1990. Located at Tan Son Nhut Airport outside of Ho Chi Minh City, the center provides temporary living quarters for over one thousand applicants at a time. This is also where the U.S. State Department interviews Amerasians to determine final approval. After spending several weeks at the center, the immigrants fly to the Philippines for six months of studying English and American culture before entering the United States.

The Transit Center has helped many Amerasians who were formerly homeless find a place to live. However, there are still many Amerasians waiting for final approval who must live with relatives, on the streets, or wherever they can. Many applicants wait as long as five years for the final journey to America.

Once resettled in the USA, the new arrivals are required to repay the U.S. government for travel and exit expenses. After five years, Amerasians can apply for citizenship. If an American father acknowledges paternity, his son or daughter automatically becomes a citizen. Chances of locating an American father, however, have proven to be very remote.

—S. G.

VIETNAMESE WORDS

There are numerous accent marks and hyphens used in Vietnamese; however, most publications written in English leave many of them off. For the sake of readability, they have been left off here as well.

ao dai	tight-fitting long tunic open on the sides and worn over billowy pants
bui-doi	dust of life
cai liem	sickle
cam on co	thank you, miss
ca-phe da	iced coffee
cat gat	cut halfway up

cat lua	close to the ground
cha gio	meat rolls
chua hoang	unwed mother
cong-vien	small park in the middle of a street intersection (traffic circle with a park)
con-hoang	illegitimate child
con-lai	half-breed
cyclo	French term for three-wheeled bicycle with a passenger seat in front of a driver
don ganh	bamboo pole carried over one shoulder
dong	Vietnamese unit of money (50 *dong* = 1 cent)
giong	strips hanging from *don ganh* to form a cradle for baskets
lam co lua di	first weeding of the paddies
Lien-xo	Soviet Union

long-den	paper lantern used in the Moon Festival
lua giong	rice used as seed
lua lep	darkened rice
moi	mountain tribesman; also called Montagnards (insulting term, means "savage")
nha duoi	back of Vietnamese house
nha tren	front of Vietnamese house
non-la	cone-shaped hat
nuoc chanh	lemonade/limeade
nuoc mam	fish sauce
nuoc mia	sugarcane juice
pho	rice noodles, or rice noodle soup
quan	pants
tam-ban	flat-bottomed skiff usually propelled by two oars

tai chi	an ancient Chinese discipline of meditative movements used as a system of exercises
Têt Trung-thu	Mid-Autumn Festival, Moon Festival
ty-ba	an old musical instrument
Xo-Viet	Soviet (person)

FRANKLIN PIERCE COLLEGE LIBRARY

00070207

DATE DUE

MAY 0 1 2001			
AUG 2 6 2011			
GAYLORD			PRINTED IN U.S.A.